I WANT TO LOVE YOU IN EVERY KIND OF WAY

BRII TAYLOR

TEXT UCP TO 22828 TO SUBSCRIBE TO OUR MAILING LIST
If you would like to join our team, submit the first 3-4 chapters of your completed manuscript to
Submissions@UrbanChapterspublications.com

Acknowledgments

First, I give all honor and glory to God for blessing me with this gift. I want to use it how He gave it to me to use. Sometimes I stand in my own way and get stuck in my head. By praying and pushing past the nothing, I get through by the grace of God. This is my third year being an author, and I'm seeing the things I prayed for in my first year. I never thought I'd even be a published author. This was only a dream I've had since I was twelve. So, I thank Him.

To my beautiful/dope publisher, sister and mentor, Jahquel J. Ahh, it's been three years since you took me under your wing. You know three is one of God's numbers, right? As I was writing this book, I thought about how far I've come since book one. I thought about the day I came to your inbox, and you were so nice and informative. You could've turned me away, but nope! You even told me you could recommend other publishers before you told me you were one yourself. You have always been so dope and inspirational to me. Even three years down the road, you got the same energy. You keep it real with me, motivate me to the fullest, and challenge me to be the best Brii I can be. I love and appreciate you for that. Thank you for all that you do/have done. I love you, Jah baby!

To my parents, I love y'all so much! Y'all are always there for when I need you. You guys are TRUE examples. My prayer is that one day I can give back all that you guys have given me.

To my siblings, I love y'all so much! My prayer for y'all is that you all follow your dreams. Never let fear stand in the way of what you're after.

To my readers, THANK YOU! I love you so much for continuing to rock with me.

Let's Connect!
FACEBOOK: BRII TAYLOR

Facebook Page: Ms. Brii
Facebook Group: Ms. Brii's Reader's Group
Instagram: everything_ms.brii
Twitter: taylor_brii
SC: Bribby_monroe
Website: www.msbrii.com
Email: briitaylorwrites@gmail.com

Listen to the book playlist!
Apple Music: https://itunes.apple.com/us/playlist/i-want-to-love-you-in-every-kind-of-way/pl.u-V9D7vdJiBoq5D1J

Sometimes love comes at you fast and hard…To my mama, Kakieba Taylor— Lady, you are appreciated! ♥☐

Santana Janae Jackson

"Welcome to *Juwelz*. How can we help you today?"

"I saw this flyer at the bus stop. I brought my son to get a haircut." I held the flyer that read *'free back to school haircuts @Juwelz'* with the address to this barber shop enlisted.

The woman who greeted me switched over from behind the counter and took the flyer from my hands. I noticed how thick in the hips and thighs, yet so small in the waist she was. Most women would kill for the curves she possessed, and here she was looking like a beautifully molded together Coke bottle. Adding to her appearance, making her that much more envied, she was a warm caramel tone, blemish free, and was beautiful in the face. Her face was smooth. Her almond shaped eyes were brown and slanted, making her appearance exotic. Her lips were small and pouty, painted a shiny pink.

"Oh, girl, we already did this. The last day was Tuesday. See?" She pointed her long French tip acrylics at the dates that were on the flyer. That was two days ago.

Damn. "Okay, thank you so much. Come on, Ma— boy! Get down from there!"

"Mommy, watch this!" He jumped down from the black coffee table he was standing on.

"Malik! Get over here, now!" I stormed over to him and snatched him up by his collar. "I told you when we got here—"

"Whoa, whoa, whoa! Aye, love, let him go, aight?" I heard a deep voice call out from behind me. I turned around, snapping my head in his direction. For a second, I got lost in his looks. His piercing light brown eyes, medium brown skin, and his full and thick lips to be exact. The way his thick eyebrows were furrowed and eyes penetrating me was like he was gazing into my soul.

"Excuse me?" I found my words, attitude and all.

"I said…" he sauntered over to me. "Let little man go. He didn't do nothing wrong."

"Um, this is my son. You can't tell me what to do with him." I returned the deep mug he was giving me.

"Well this is my shop, and I don't want to see any child being mistreated."

"Well we're leaving your shop, so you won't have to see—hold up! *Mistreated?* Ain't nobody mistreating him. He's obviously using your table as a diving board, and I'm stopping him so you won't have to buy another table."

"Obviously, he's a kid and I don't give a— you know what?" He stopped talking, licked his lips, and took a deep breath. "Aye, little man, come have a seat in my chair."

"What? Malik, no! We're leaving." I reached for his hand. The guy reached for his other hand. I pulled him away in time so he couldn't touch him. I turned to leave only to feel my feet being lifted off the ground.

"What the— what!"

"Aye, love, calm down, aight?" He set me in the chair and kneeled in front of me. "I'm going to give your little

2

man a haircut. You just sit here and calm down. Whatever is stressing you out, pray it off and by the—"

"Are you—"

"*And by the time I'm done*, you should be good… aight?" His light brown eyes had turned a shade darker. I found myself gazing into them and nodding my head at him.

"What makes you think I'm stressed?" I found the courage to ask. I was going to keep my protest up and walk out with my son in tow. Clearly, that wasn't going to happen, so I may as well chill and do what this man said.

"I can see it in your shoulders, face, and eyes. You tense as I don't know what. You work a lot?" he queried.

I nodded my head, saying yes. "I work and I'm in school."

"What you in school for?" As long as he'd been kneeled down on the floor, I knew his legs and knees had to hurt by now. Still, he stayed low enough so I could look down into his eyes and make eye contact.

"I'm in nursing school."

"How much longer you got?"

"A year."

"How old are you?"

"Twenty-five. How old are you?"

"Twenty-seven. What's your name?"

"Santana. What's your name?"

"Julius." He held his hand out for me to shake. Extending my hand, I shook his. "Everybody calls me Juwelz though."

"Okay… Juwelz."

Finally, he stood up. "Aight, love. Give me some time, and I'll have your little man hooked up." He started to walk away, but I called to him.

"I don't have any money to—"

"It's on the house, love." He winked with a half smile,

3

turned on the heels of his Timbs, and swaggered over to the direction of my son.

Malik was already set up in the chair with a cloak around him. I shook my head at him spinning in the chair. When he was three, the doctors diagnosed him with ADHD. I refused to believe that my son, *a three-year-old toddler* at the time, had ADHD. I mean, he was three. He was supposed to be active. I called him a curious kid that liked to get into stuff.

So when the doctors tried to prescribe him with some medicine, I told him where he could take that prescription and left the doctor's office. Needless to say, I switched doctors. Malik was now eight.

His current doctor has tried to get me to "understand" that my son is extremely hyper, even for his age, and recommend I start giving him Ritalin. As bad as I wanted to switch or sue these doctors for "misdiagnosing" my child when I didn't ask them to, I understood they were only doing their jobs. Watching him fidget in the chair now made me wonder if those doctors were right. Did my son have ADHD?

Lord, I am tired as I don't know what. I feel like giving up sometimes. I know that's not an option because I have a child to live for. I'm only twenty-five and feel like I've been through more than a person twice my age. God, if you can hear me... please help. I need help and don't know what to do.

Feeling my phone vibrate in my purse, I pulled it out to look at it. It was an unknown number calling. Missing the call, I waited to see if they'd leave a voicemail. I never answered unknown numbers and always waited for them to leave a message first. As soon as my phone notified me that I had a voicemail, I anxiously checked it.

"Hello, this is Sarah Reed from Visiting Angels. I was calling to get in touch with Santana Jackson. We got your application and would like for you to come in for an interview. Please call back at…"

The room felt like it was spinning, and I was floating. My mood had elevated, and I felt like getting up and dancing all around this shop. *God, you're so amazing and work fast!* This was the break I'd been looking for. I'd been working at a job that I hated for more than two years so far. It was a homecare facility. I hated the hours and the staff. Every day felt like I got into it with one of co-workers or supervisors over something I didn't do. They worked me like a dog and knew I was in school. Too many times my job was threatened to be taken away if I didn't come in, because I called in sick. Truth be told, this was the only source of income I was getting. I couldn't get food stamps because I made too much. I refused to be on welfare, so this was it. For the last month, I'd been putting in job applications to anywhere that I could get decent hours and pay. I came across Visiting Angels because my mother's next-door neighbor had a personal caregiver that worked for the company. I asked the lady that helped my mother's neighbor about the job, and she told me all I needed to know. Now I'd gotten a call back in less than two weeks.

Thank you, God! My knee bounced as I waited for someone to pick up the phone. At the same time, I had my eyes fixed on Malik and Juwelz. Malik seemed to had calmed down, and they looked to be in a deep conversation. Though I wanted to know what this man could've been telling my baby, I was happy that Leek was being calm for a change.

Julius "Juwelz" (JEW-WELLS) Davis

"How old are you, lil' man?"

"Uh, eight. How old are you?"

"Guess." I stopped cutting little man's hair and made eye contact with him in the mirror.

"Uh, one hundred?" He giggled, placing his hand over his smile. That told me he didn't really think I was one hundred but wanted to be funny. I played along with him though.

"Dang, lil' man. That's what you think? I'm offended." I placed my hand over my chest, faking like I was hurt.

"Okay, okay, let me guess again… Thirty!" He blurted, kicking his feet, and laughing hard. I joined him in laughter, shaking my head.

"You close, but naw. I'm twenty-seven, lil' man."

"That's old!"

"Dang, it's like that?" I chucked. "What grade you in? First grade?"

"I'm going to third grade!" he told me like I was already supposed to know.

"Aw, my bad. What you want to be when you grow up?"

"I want to be like Steph Curry when I grow up." He moved his arms like he was swishing and dunking a ball.

"Aight, aight. That's what's up. I used to want to be a basketball player when I was your age. You like the Trail Blazers?"

He started bouncing in his seat. "Rip City! Rip City! Rip City! Ayyye!"

"Ayyye!" I stopped cutting to dance with him. I was just bouncing my shoulders and bobbing my head.

"I wish I can go to a real game. That would be so fun! I just watch the game at my granny house though." He shrugged.

"We watch the game here at the shop too. You welcome to come and watch it."

"Cool! I'll ask my mommy first."

I looked over at Santana as she had her head down in her phone. She had a huge smile on her face that made me want to know what she was smiling about. Her having a man never crossed my mind, because I honestly didn't care. Nor was it my business. I was just trying to get her to calm down some. The way she snatched her son up confirmed my initial thoughts. I knew from the jump she was stressed out. She walked in looking dead tired, her hair frizzled and shoulders slumped. The hard expression on her face would scare most but not me. Even looking as stressed and burnt out as she did, she was beautiful.

She had a smooth peanut butter skin tone with small light brown freckles on her face. She was small in stature, and she appeared frail. Her eyes were a deep brown and carried so much pain. I could sense it on her along with the stress she carried. Her small but plump heart-shaped lips were just right for her face. They stuck out the most to me.

Her pointed nose could have somebody thinking she was bougie, but it was small and cute. Though her hair was untamed, it was silky and radiant, up in a bun. All she needed was a little sleep, a smile, and maybe some gel to lay her baby hairs down.

"Aight, lil' man. I'm all finished. What you think?" I handed him a hand mirror. He moved it around to both sides of his head and nodded with an approving smile. "You like it?"

"Yeah!"

"Aight. Let me take you to your mama." I helped him out the chair and walked him over to where Santana was sitting. I noticed the vibrant look she now had. Her skin was glowing compared to what it was earlier. I couldn't help but wonder what changed for her?

"Aww, you look so good! I love it! Thank you, Juwelz." She jumped to her feet with newfound energy and a big smile.

Seeing her smile caused me to smile. It also made my heart skip a beat. A refreshing chill ran through my body, and it felt like my pores had just been cleansed. "Good. I'm glad to hear that."

"I appreciate you doing this for no charge and such last minute. Please, you have to let me pay you back when I get some money," she urged, placing her hand on my upper right arm.

I shook my head in disapproval. "No can do, love. I meant what I said. This cut was on the house."

"But—"

"No."

"How about—"

"Nuh uhn."

"Well, what if—"

"Bye, Santana."

8

"Ughhh!" she groaned in defeat. "I gotta take this L then, huh?"

I smirked at the mention of her taking an L, when really, she'd just gained. She was too stubborn to realize or accept it though.

Just then, an idea popped into my head. "You really want to pay me back?"

"Yes, I do!" she exclaimed with sincerity.

"Okay, you can pay me back by going to dinner with me."

The smile on her face dropped. "Bye, Juwelz."

She turned to leave with Malik's hand in hers. I reached for her free hand and pulled her back. "I'm serious, Santana. You want to pay me back so badly... come to dinner with me."

"Naw, it's okay. I'll just take this loss. Malik, tell Juwelz bye."

"Bye, Juwelz!" He waved to me on the way, walking toward the entrance.

"See ya, lil' man! Aye, Santana, bring him back in a few weeks!" I called behind them.

Judging by the texture of his hair, Malik's hair would grow back rather quickly. If Santana wanted to keep it looking right, she'd have to bring little man back to the shop.

"Mn-mn-mm-mn-mn!" My cousin/receptionist, Cynthia, grunted, shaking her head.

"What you shaking that bobble head at?" I joked, leaning against the counter. She was going over the books for the shop like she normally did when it was nearing closing time. Between my three barbers and one beautician, my beautician and one of my barbers had one more client to do before closing time.

"You, big head boy. You think I didn't see your

shooting your shot to *Santana*? Mhm, you ain't slick, asking her to go to dinner as payment." She snickered, shaking her head. Not once did she lose count.

Cynthia had gone to school for accounting—Everest College to be exact. She was in her last year when the school got sued and had to close down. My cousin was devastated because she had paid a lot of my money to do a two-year course. The sad part about it, she couldn't even take the credits she obtained from Everest and go to Port-land Community College or Mount Hood. There was a blessing in all this though. She received all the payments she'd made to Everest back.

Instead of going back to school, she asked me if she could just work in the shop. Of course I didn't deny or turn her away. Though I did encourage her to go back to school, I was glad for the help.

"Whatever. I wasn't shooting nothing. I was being for real with her." I can't lie like my feelings didn't get stung from Santana shooting me down. I mean, I didn't expect her to say yes anyways. She probably had a man or something.

"Yeah, okay. But be careful with her. You don't know if she got a man or nothing." Cyn was reading my mind, but I wouldn't admit it.

"Anyways... how's it looking?" I was referring to the books.

"It's great! The shop has been doing really well lately. I admit, sometimes I'm surprised to see how many people are willing to travel all this way just to get a haircut." She giggled.

"Ohhh, you got jokes, huh?" I chuckled. Cyn thought she was funny.

"Nooo! I'm just playing, Ju-Ju Bean. I know you dope

with them clippers, and you have the best barbers and stylists," she genuinely complimented.

"Aww, thanks, bobble head." I chin checked her, and she swatted at my hand but missed.

"Ohh, you gotta be quicker than that!" I continued to joke with her for a few minutes more.

Truth be told, Cyn was more like my little sister than cousin. We practically grew up together. We both were the only children of our parents. Her mom and my dad were brother and sister. There were plenty of times where I'd stay and visit her house and vice versa.

"How's Unk doing?" Her tone turned serious.

"He's doing aight. Taking it one day at a time, you know?"

"Yeah, that's good. I got to come by and see about him." Cyn giggled to lighten the mood.

I offered a small smile. "Yeah, you do… I'm going to be in the back if y'all need me."

Talking about my dad always made me emotional. Just a year ago, we found out he had MS. Of course, I took it hard because I never imagined my father being in the state he was in. The man that I once knew to walk big and tall was now using a cane to walk. Half the time he could barely stand. There were times when it was hard for him to form his words and sentences. There were good days and bad days. We were told he would need a caregiver in the long run. I was doing the caregiving at first. I'd go to his apartment and set up his meds, clean up his kitchen, bedroom, and living room, and cook his meals. That got tiring, so eventually, I moved him into my four bedroom, three and a half bath home.

I thought it would be easier to have him home with me. However, it turned out to be more work than I imagined. I knew I would need help sooner or later. At first, I couldn't afford to hire a caregiver to care for him while I was at work. I also didn't want to put him in a home. I heard horror stories about how people were treated in homes. I'd be damned if my dad was being mistreated. So I suffered until I could afford to hire someone.

I ended up finding an agency that was reasonable in price, and I loved their name: *Visiting Angels*. So far, their service had been exceptional and consistent. I loved that they met my dad's and my expectations. We didn't want a bunch of different faces, so they'd been having the same lady, Brittany, come for the last six months now. The only time we got somebody new was when Brittany was either sick or on vacation.

An hour went by, and I was happy to be closing *Juwelz*. It felt good to have a business that was doing well. Since I was a kid, I wanted to own my own business. I never imagined it would be a barber shop. I thought it'd be a food truck or restaurant. I loved to cut hair, but cooking was my first love. While I was attending Portland State, I considered also enrolling in culinary school. I was in school for business marketing and finance management. I went the whole way and obtained a master's degree. There was a lot of stuff I could do with my degree, and I chose to manage my own shop.

While I was in college, I struggled with money, as most students do. I was still living at home with my parents. I was always good with the clippers, so I would cut hair in my mama's kitchen. My mama would always playfully threaten to turn me in for cutting hair illegally in her kitchen. She would also encourage me to get a barber's license and open a shop. It wasn't until my mother passed away that I went ahead and honored her words. I vowed to never cut hair without a license again. So here I was, owning my own shop.

~&~

"What's up, old man? What you watching?" I greeted my dad on the way in the house. He was sitting up in his La-Z-Boy with his feet up. This was his favorite spot in the house.

"H-hey, son!" His eyes lit up when he noticed me standing there.

I went over and kissed his forehead like I always did when I came in. "Where's Brittany?"

"Hey, Juwelz!" I heard that familiar, chipper voice. Brittany was a young and sweet soul. She was nineteen and going to Portland State University. I loved that we had that in common. It gave us something to talk about at dinner. I usually cooked after I was showered and settled in good. Brittany left at nine, after she tucked my dad into bed. It was such a relief for me, because then I could just relax.

"Hey, Brittany. How are you? I'm going to get some dinner going in a few."

"I'm good! How was your day? I don't mind cooking dinner tonight," she happily offered.

"Long and tiring... Naw, it's cool. I want to cook. It helps me to relieve my stress." I refused her, as I always did.

"Okay. Well let me know if you need anything..."

"Cool."

It took me less than thirty minutes to get showered and changed into something comfortable. I couldn't wait to get in the kitchen and make the recipe I found on Pinterest earlier. It was stuffed chicken Marsala. I planned to cook garlic mashed potatoes and asparagus with it. For dessert, I had half a lemon pound cake with orange glaze I had baked earlier in the week.

Brittany came bouncing into the kitchen as I was

halfway done with dinner. "Oh! I wanted to tell you… I won't be here as much in the next couple of weeks. With school getting started, I want to focus more on that than work…"

I could hear the sadness behind her voice. I didn't want her to feel bad about choosing her education over work. What kind of a person would I be? "That's alright. I understand. Put your studies first always. Never apologize about that."

"I hear you. I just didn't want you to be upset."

"I'm not upset. I'm sure whoever comes to take your place won't be as good, but it's all good. Thanks for telling me." I smiled at her.

She smiled back. "No problem. Thank you for under-standing."

I told Brittany I wasn't upset, and I wasn't. I was just anxious to meet the person that would be filling in on the days she wasn't here. I only met two other caregivers besides her. They were cool and all, but knowing who was in my house was a must for me.

Lord, send a true angel…

3

Santana

"Are you going to be back home tonight or tomorrow morning?" Hearing the disappointment in my son's voice crushed my spirit. He was used to me going to work in the morning and not being home until late at night or early the next morning. Between work and school, this is what I dealt with.

"No, baby. Mommy will be home tonight. I got a new job, and I don't have to work as many hours anymore," I proudly told him.

I was grateful and relieved to have quit my old job and was now working for Visiting Angels. The last two weeks, things had been smooth with them. I spent one day doing orientation, and I'd been working since then. So far, I'd been working with this nice elderly lady, from nine in the morning 'til six in the evening. I worked with her three days out the week, Monday, Tuesday, and Friday. The rest of my week had been free.

Today, I was starting a new client I agreed to work with twice a week—Wednesday and Thursday. The office was trying to get me to give up my lady and work with this man five days a week. I told them no because his shift was from nine in the morning to nine at night. I felt crazy enough taking that on two days in a row. There was no way I was doing it for five days. Besides that, I was getting used to getting home to Leek after six versus ten o'clock at night or midnight.

"Okay, Mommy. I'll miss you, but I know you're doing this for my good and so I can have what I want and need." My baby recited what I'd told him what felt like a thousand times. It brought tears to my eyes to hear him say it. *Thank you, God, for my son.*

"Yes, baby, that's right." I choked up on my tears. Looking into my son's big, dark brown eyes, I searched for his understanding, and you know what? I found it. Leek knew I had to work, and it was all for him to have a good life. I silently complained about all the work I had to do all the time. The real truth was, I didn't mind it as much as I complained. It was all for him—my son.

I was seventeen and just out of high school when I had Malik. A lot of people, including my own family, turned their backs on me. Other than my mama, I had nobody. Friends that I thought were real turned out not to be. They fled as soon as they heard I was pregnant. Not even Malik's donor or his family wanted anything to do with me.

Malik's donor, Isaac, was a preacher's kid. As soon as I told him I was pregnant, he begged me to get rid of the baby. It was either that or disassociate myself from him. Meaning, don't tell nobody he was my baby daddy. Of course I wasn't aborting my child, so I disassociated myself from Isaac.

At first, I was mad, hurt, and depressed. I was forced to lie to my family and say I didn't know who my child's father was. I was looked at as a hoe. That's what drove them to turn their backs, I believe. Meanwhile, Isaac was carrying on like everything was all good in his world. He had a new girlfriend within a month, and I was a distant memory—that's what hurt the most.

Last I heard from him, I was on Facebook and saw he had moved to California. He was engaged and about to have a baby with someone else. I couldn't say that I wasn't hurt, because I was. He couldn't claim my baby, but he could claim his fiancée's?

Knock! Knock!

"Grandma's here!" Malik ran out the bathroom and to the front door of our small apartment. It might've been small, but it was ours.

"Hey, GG's baby!" I heard my mother's voice from the bathroom. I finished combing my hair so I could go and greet her.

"Grandma, you wanna see the new clothes Mommy got me?" He was referring to the brand-new clothes I'd gotten him for school. Leek was starting kindergarten next week, and I couldn't be any more excited. I was also nervous for my baby. Given the false diagnosis these doctors were trying to give him, I worried how he'd do in class. I wondered if he'd make any friends and stuff like that. I'd be damned if my baby was singled out for whatever reason. I was the type of mom that would go to war over mine.

"Yes, baby. Go get them." She nodded with a smile deeply embedded in her face. As Malik ran past me to the back, I traveled in the opposite direction, into my mama's opened arms.

"Hey, Mommy!" I squeezed my arms around her as she did the same to me. Being in her arms made me feel like everything would be okay. When I was a little girl, I didn't appreciate her hugs as much. Now I craved them.

"Hey, baby. How are you?" She pulled away and kissed me on the cheek.

"I'm good! I'm happy that I got this new job. I don't know how I would've survived any longer in that facility. I'm also happy I quit the right way and didn't just walk out." Had I walked out instead of giving a two-week notice, I wouldn't have gotten paid all the vacation and time off hours I'd accumulated. I would've left with just the hours I'd worked within that pay period.

Due to me never going on vacation and barely using any of my time off, my last check was… well, blessed! I was able to pay two months' rent, buy my son a bunch of new stuff, and I got some new stuff for the apartment. The rest of the money, I split between Leek's trust fund and my "get a car" money pool.

"That's great, baby. When you coming back to church? It's been two years' worth of Sundays. You don't work on Sundays anymore now, baby. You could come and pay your own tithes… Give God praise for the blessings he poured and still pouring down in your life."

I knew it was coming. It never ceased. My mother wanted me to come to church so badly. Honestly, I'd been wanting to go too. However, I always had work on Sundays. Any Sunday I didn't work, I was too tired to get out of bed. I did pay my tithes though. I would send them through my mother.

"You're right, Mama. It's time for me to come back. I have no excuse not to go now." Every day, I thanked God for that. I prayed for what I wanted in a job, and he gave me exactly that.

"Oh, that's so great to hear, baby! Everybody will be so happy to see you!"

"Yeah, me too, Mommy." I half smiled.

I couldn't lie like I wasn't a little nervous to go back to

church. This was the church I'd been going to since I was a small child. For them to see me now, all grown up with a kid and not married? It was a bit nerve racking. I knew this was something I shouldn't be worried about, given that you were supposed to come as you are. They say that, but there was always somebody in the back judging you.

~&~

Inhale… exhale…
Knock. Knock. Knock.

"Good morning, my name is Santana. I'm here from Visiting Angels. I'll be your caregiver today…" I recited the lines I was given during orientation. This was only my second time having to say this. I'd established a bond with my other client, so she knew when I was coming and what I was there for.

Knock. Knock. Knock.

"I hope I'm at the right house." Pulling my phone out of my purse, I checked the address. This was the right address. Nobody was coming to the door yet though.

From my understanding, the guy had MS, but he could still get around. Then again, the agency told me that he lived with his son, and he was going to be here to meet and greet with me. Maybe his son forgot.

I was raising my hand to knock again, when I heard the door locks being moved. *Okay San, you got this, girl. Just go in here and get the job done.* I had to give myself a little motivational pep talk.

"Good morning, my name is Santana, and I'm here from—" Looking up from my phone and seeing his face caused me to pause in the middle of my sentence. "Juwelz… w-what are you doing here?"

I hated that sexy yet cocky smirk of his so much. I only

met this man a few weeks ago but couldn't get it out of my mind. Him. I couldn't get him out of my mind. I saw his face in my dreams, and that stupid smirk would be resting on his face.

"Good morning, love," he coolly replied. Ugh! I hated how he called me "love". I loved it too though. Was that even possible?

"Good morning. What are you doing here?" I shifted all my weight to one leg and placed my hands on my hips.

He mimicked my gesture and rolled his neck, replying, "I live here, woman. What are you doing here?"

I fought it, but the smile I didn't want to smile cracked my lips apart and penetrated my dimples. "I was sent here from an agency called *Visiting Angels*. Unless they gave me the wrong address…"

"Nope, this is the right address. Come on in. I was just about to make breakfast. You can join me and Pops." He moved to the side to let me in the house. I was a little nervous to walk in. The thought of me meeting this man weeks ago at his shop and now I was at his house, was eating at me. "You coming inside, love?"

"Yeah… I'm coming."

Dear, Lord, what did you get me into?

4

Juwelz

"Is the food nasty, love?" I asked Santana, watching her poke at the veggie omelette I had prepared for her. She'd taken a few bites of her toast, but that was it. I admit, she was offending me a little.

She cleared her throat, pushing the plate away. "Um, no. It's delicious. It's just that, the agency said that we're not supposed to eat the clients' food. I don't mean to offend you..." she sweetly apologized.

"Ahh, okay, I see. Well, I cook for all my father's care-givers all the time. The agency knows and should have informed you." I didn't mean to come off rudely. I was just telling her how it was. Now, I wouldn't force her to eat my cooking, if she truly didn't want to eat it. She should have been informed that this was what I did. Most of the care-givers appreciated it.

"I said I didn't mean to offend you, sheesh." She smirked, pulling her plate back in front of her and digging into the omelette. "Maybe I missed that section of the care plan."

"Yeah, maybe." I scoffed. She snickered as she

continued to eat. I knew I was probably acting like a big baby, but I couldn't help it. I took pride in my cooking skills.

"Do you need help with that, Mr. Davis?" Santana reached in to grab my father's knife and fork to help cut his food up. He looked up and smiled at her. Noticing the twinkle in his eye, I could tell he was taking a liking to her already. He hadn't said much to her since she came in the house, but I peeped him gawking at her every move. His face never switched from the goofy grin on his face.

"You can call me JD," he clearly spoke. In his stage of MS, he was starting to stutter out some of his words. He would have to take his time to say certain things sometimes. I was always patient with him. This was the first time I heard him talk so smoothly.

"Aww, okay, JD. You can call me San." Santana smiled lovingly at him.

"How old are you, San?" he asked, sitting up straight in his chair. Well I'll be damned. My dad was trying to get his mack on. If he knew any better, he'd back off. I had my eyes on her first.

"I'm twenty-five." San giggled. "Are you originally from Portland?"

"No, I'm from Michigan. After I served in World War II, I moved out here. I settled down with my wife, and we had this knuckle head." He laughed. "Do you have kids?"

I watched San's eyes light up when she started talking about Malik. "Yes, I have a son. His name is Malik, he's eight, and a handful. I always joke with him and my mom that he's two kids in one. I don't need anymore."

"But you do want more, right?" I butted into their conversation. Both my dad and San stopped to turn their heads at me. San had a surprised look on her face. My dad

22

looked at me like he did when I was a kid. Like I was inter-rupting grown folks' business.

"Um... I don't know. I might if the right one comes along. Then again, I have Malik, and he's a handful. He's more than enough," she explained.

"Well what if your new man wants more kids? Of course, being that he accepts Malik as his own. Is that something you'd be willing to consider?"

I watched her facial expression change positions as she thought about my question. "*If*, and only *if* I ever decide to settle down and get a man... then, yeah... I'll consider having more kids."

That's all I needed to hear as I nodded my head in her direction. Briefly, she held eye contact and then directed her attention toward my dad. "So, JD..."

Finishing my breakfast, I sat and just listened to them engage in conversation. Occasionally, I'd join them in laughter if something was funny. I didn't dare interrupt with my own questions again. I heeded the way my dad stared at me earlier. I didn't want no smoke.

~&~

"Aye, man, what's up with your cousin? Be real with me. She like women or something?" my boy/barber Aaron asked me as he was cutting a client's hair. I had just finished with my last appointment and was sweeping my station. I was taking walk-ins for the rest of the day.

"Man, Cyn don't like women. I know this for a fact." I shook my head, chuckling at his silly question.

"Then what's up with her? She won't look a brother's way for nothing. I be giving her compliments and trying to spark conversation. Man, look... I bought her lunch on a couple occasions. She still treating me like the brother she always wanted. Is there a big *I just want to be your homie* sign on my forehead or something?"

"Aye, man, chill… You a little too close to my ear," his client fussed, flinching in the chair. I tried not to laugh but it was funny.

"Aye, man, chill out before Greg here won't have an ear," I joked. Greg didn't find anything funny. In fact, he side-eyed me and grunted. "Look, A… I know you're a good guy—deep, deep, deep, deep, deep—"

"Aye, man, chill. I get it." A stopped cutting and pointed his clippers in my direction.

"*Like I said*, you a good guy and all. I'm sure Cyn thinks so too…"

"But?" He raised his eyebrow.

"But, man… how can I put this?" I scratched my head. "You the player type, bro."

"The player type? What that even mean?"

"It means that you always pulling up with a different dip, man," one of the other barbers Sean jumped in the conversation. He was laughing and shaking his head. "Cyn don't want to be on your list of women you use, dawg."

"What? I don't use women!" Aaron denied.

As soon as he said that, the shop grew quiet. Everybody was giving him a side eye. Next, the entire shop erupted into a fit of laughter.

Aaron knew he was wrong for trying to court my cousin. He stayed pulling up in a different female's car. I worried about him doing that sometimes, but I remained in my lane. As long as he didn't bring his drama into the shop, it wasn't my business.

"Look, all I'm going to say is… *I don't wanna be a player no more!*" A sang "Still Not A Player" all offkey.

Again, we were all cracking up at Aaron's antics. This was an everyday thing with us. It was always fun and games in the shop. There was never a dull moment. This place was like a home away from home. It was full of good vibes, hard work, and likeminded people.

Ding!

"Heeey, Cyn!" everyone greeted as she walked through the door. She wore a smile and carried a big pink box in her arms.

I already knew it was a box of donuts. This was what Cyn did. She brought food and snacks to the shop so we all wouldn't be famished throughout the day. She also kept everything stocked in the back and was a hell of a good saleswoman. She got new people in this shop almost every day. If she ever got tired of accounting, she could trade that in and go into sales.

"Ju-Ju Bean, can you help me with this stuff in the back?" she asked on her way past my station. I wasn't doing nothing, so I didn't mind.

When I got to the back, she was standing there with her arms folded and a smug smirk on her face. Now I had the feeling she didn't really need my help. She was up to something though.

"Why you giving me that look? What do you want, Cyn?" I knew it was something.

"Mhm, I do want something." She grinned.

"And what's that?" I asked inquisitively.

"I want to know what's really up with you and *San*?" She put emphasis on Santana's nickname, cheesing hard as ever. Taking a deep breath in then out, I leaned against the wall. I couldn't stop myself from smiling too.

"I see you went to see your uncle."

She nodded her head. "Mhm, I did. So, how did you pull it off, Juwelz?"

I gave her a confused look because I was truly confused. "Pull what off?"

"Boy, don't play dumb. How did you get her over your house to take care of Uncle? Was this a part of the *payback*?"

"Payback—girl, no!" I had to laugh at my cousin for thinking such a thing. "For your information, Santana showed up to my door this morning. She's Pops' new caregiver. Brittany won't be around so much anymore, so the agency found a new angel to fill in on the days she won't be there."

"Oohhh, I see, and a true angel they found. I know it's too soon to say, but I love San! Uncle loves her too. I've never seen him be so talkative, and his words are flowing out so well! She's good for him… for you too."

"How you figure she's good for me?" Though I felt something for San and felt she could be a good match, I wanted to hear my cousin's thoughts about her.

"She has a good head on her shoulders, from what I could tell when I visited today. She's smart, funny, nice, and a true caregiver. I like how patient she is, and I can see true colors off bat. You know how some people seem like they real but you can see right through it?" she paused to ask. I nodded in agreement. I didn't know many people who weren't solid, which was how I could distinguish who was and wasn't. "Well, she's not like that. I know it's too soon or whatever, but I got a good feeling about San."

I had a good feeling about San too. She seemed standoffish when it came to me, but I was sure within time, that would change.

Lord, give me a true sign…

5

Santana

Sunday...

"*Welcome into this place. Welcome into this broken vessel. You desire to abide in the praises of your people. So we lift our hands and lift our hearts. As we offer up this praise unto your name...*"

Being in church for the first time in such a long time, I felt like a foreigner amongst the people. I saw so many familiar faces. I also saw so many new faces. Well, faces that I hadn't met before. These people had probably been going to this church for all of the two years I'd been gone.

Closing my eyes, I listened to the song and let the words sink in. It had been so long since I heard it, I forgot the lyrics. I did feel what the words were sanding though.

"*So we lift our hands and we lift our hearts. As we offer up this praise unto your name...*"

Before I knew it, my hands were in the air, and tears were rapidly running down my face. All I could think about was where I was just two years ago to where I am now. I was seeing the blessings that I took for granted all this time.

The next thing I felt were my mother's warms hands

rubbing my back as I continued to praise God. It was so funny because I promised myself, and even joked with my mama on the way to church, that I wouldn't do this. My plan was to just walk in and smile and clap my hands a little, pay my offering, listen to the preacher talk, then go home. Yet, here I was.

"He sees you, baby. God sees you, and He loves you. As long as you give him the glory and praise in everything, He will keep blessing you." My mother cooed into my ear. "Just surrender to Him, baby. You don't have to carry the load anymore. He got you... Yes, Lord."

"Yes, Lord..." I cried harder, hearing everything my mother just told me. It was like she had an extra look into my life. My soul. Like she knew my life, other than what I told her.

Yes, Lord.

Once church was over, I felt relieved. Knowing God was taking care of me and everything was working for my good had me in on a new wave. I was on a natural high, on a cloud of my own. I was hugging people I hadn't seen in so long and people I'd never met. There were a few childhood friends that came up and were happy to see me as well. I was surprised because these were the same women who turned their noses up at me when I got pregnant. Oh well, I guess time changed things.

"San, baby, come over here. I want you to meet someone." I heard my mama call for me. I was silently thanking God because I was tired of standing in a circle with a group of fake women. No matter how happy they acted to see me, I didn't feel the vibe. I also observed the "secret" side eyes and snickers. I wasn't letting it get in my head though.

"Julius, this is my daughter—"

"San, what's up, baby girl?" Juwelz cut my mother off, taking initiative, and pulling me into a hug.

I wouldn't lie like he didn't smell good and look good. He was dressed in some blue fitted jeans and a black fitted shirt with some shiny loafers. His hair looked like it was freshly lined up, and his eyebrows were manicured.

"Hey, Juwelz... How are you?" I shyly spoke, pulling away from him. I quickly glanced around to see if anyone noticed us hug. I was thankful that everyone seemed to be wrapped into their own conversations.

"I'm good, love, and how about yourself? You look really pretty today," he complimented, checking me out from head to toe. I was wearing a white dress with black print flowers patterned all over it. I put the dress together with some red four-inch heels. My hair was pressed out to its natural length and looking silky. Deep down, I knew I was looking good. I felt good too.

"Today?"

"Well, you look nice every day. Just today—I never seen you all dressed up."

"This is only your fourth time seeing me, though, Ju." Shortening his nickname and creating my own for him just came about. He didn't seem to have a problem with it, so I guess it was fine.

"Well, yeah, I know, but—"

"Chill, I'm only joking." I giggled. I loved to mess with him. He either got upset or nervous. It was cute.

"Did I miss something? Y'all met already?" My mama butted into our conversation. We turned our attention to her.

"Mother Jackson, I apologize for being rude. This is the woman I was just telling you about," Juwelz nervously explained. My mother glanced from me to him as her eyes lit up.

"Oh! Well, my word. Let me get out of you all's way then. I think Pastor is calling me anyway." She kissed me and then him on the cheek and scurried off.

"Umm…" Juwelz rubbed the back of his neck.

"So what did you tell her about me?" I smirked at him.

"I um, just told her how you be taking good care of my pops. He's been in better spirits since you came around. I actually think he likes you better than Brittany." He lightly chuckled. I could tell I was making him nervous.

"Oh, okay. Aww. That's nice to know. I didn't know I had such an influence in JD's life." It made me feel good to know that I made my client happy. That meant I was doing my job right.

"Yeah, he's not the only one that likes you though."

I paused as a rush of chills erupted through me. "Juwelz—"

"Cyn. Cyn likes you as well." He cut me off with that smirk I loved to hate so much. "Ever since she saw you at my place and how you was with my dad, she's been raving about you."

I admit I felt both a sense of embarrassment and relief. Both had their own reasons. "Aww, I really like her too. The few times I met her, she's been really sweet."

"Yeah…"

"Yeah…"

A moment of silence passed us as we stood there, just staring into each other's eyes. I was getting hypnotized, staring into his beautiful, light brown eyes. The way his lips were slightly parted had me feelings things I didn't think were right to be feeling in front of this church house.

"So, where is—"

"Will you go out with me, San?" he blurted, cutting me off. I was just about to ask him where his dad was.

"Um, huh?" I heard him, but I was using this as a way to rack my brain for a way to let him down gently.

By the way he kissed his teeth and cut his eyes, I could tell he was getting upset. I'd seen him do this a couple of times now. The one time when I was explaining why I wouldn't eat his cooking. The other time was when I insisted on cooking dinner for JD, but he quickly shut me down. His excuse was that he enjoyed cooking for his father after a long day of work.

"San, you heard me. I want to take you out, and I won't take no for an answer." He stepped into my personal space. I wanted so bad to take a step away from him. However, I was enjoying the way he smelled. I mean, even his breath smelled right.

"Well then, I'm sorry to say this then, Juwelz. I can't go out with you. I mean, I would love to, but you're my client's son. How would that look? What if the agency found out?" I liked Ju and all. I wanted to get to know him, more than I let on. Yet I wasn't willing to risk my work for him. My livelihood. My son's livelihood. I just couldn't. This man didn't know me from Adam or Eve. He wasn't going to take care of us if I lost my job. Nor would I let him do so.

"I understand this, but—"

"No buts, Ju… I can't go out with you. The furthest we can go is being friends. I know you want more; don't deny it." I looked into his eyes, *praying* he wanted more even though he couldn't have it. It was comforting to know that he liked me more than friends.

"Okay. I respect your wishes. Have a great evening, San." He then did something I wasn't expecting. He leaned down and gave me a kiss on the forehead before completely turning and walking away.

~&~

The week was passing by quickly and with ease. Malik had started school and was doing well. Each night, I prayed over my baby so that he did well in class. It'd only been two days so far, but that still counted, right?

Getting up, I did my usual thing and got my hygiene together before I showered and got dressed for work. I always did my thing first to give Leek extra time to sleep. Even though I didn't accept the diagnosis, I read up on kids with ADHD. Apparently, lack of sleep could affect their mood, making it harder for them to concentrate and to act up. That was any kid, adults too though.

Once I was finished, I went and got my baby up. He did his usual fussing routine for a few minutes and then got up. I got him together, in the shower, dressed, and fed him breakfast. Once I dropped him off to school, I headed to JD's house. I was a little nervous and excited. Nervous because I turned Ju down on Sunday. Excited because I missed JD. Was it weird to miss someone you'd just met?

As I pulled into the driveway, I signed into the app to clock in. I was confused when I didn't see a schedule for JD to clock into. My heart beat sped up, and my stomach began to churn as I thought the worst.

"Visiting Angels, this is Courtney. How may I direct your call?"

"Good morning, Courtney. This is Santana Jackson."

"Good morning, Santana! What can I do for you today?"

"Uh, I'm at my client, JD's house. I went to clock in, but there is no schedule to sign in. Is this a mistake?" My knee bounced as my brain started thinking all sorts of things. What if something happened to JD? *Oh no. Please, God. Please let him be alright!* I prayed.

32

"Um, no, there is no mistake. He is no longer your client, Santana. Didn't you get a call on Monday?"

"No! I didn't receive a message, no call, or nothing!"

"Okay, Santana—"

"Okay, nothing! I don't see how nobody called me and told me something. I could have stayed in bed if I knew I didn't have to be here. Why don't I have him anymore?" At this point, I was pissed. No. Pissed wasn't even the word for how I felt right now.

I woke up on the right side of the bed and expected everything to go right too. Now this just ruined my whole day!

"I'm sorry for the misunderstanding, Santana. I'm also sorry to say that I can't tell you why you're not on the schedule anymore." Even though I was raising my voice, Courtney kept hers at an even and polite tone.

"You can't tell me because it's against policy, or you can't tell me because you're not allowed to?" Usually it was because they couldn't tell us. In her case, I didn't know what it was.

"I actually don't know. I can transfer you to Karen, and she can tell you more." Before I could respond, I heard the commercial thingy come on and knew I was on hold.

"Hello, this is Karen." She cheerfully came onto the line. Clearing my throat, I calmed myself down. Karen was my supervisor, and I didn't want to come at her any type of way. That didn't excuse my behavior with Courtney. I owed her an apology. Poor thing. She didn't know a thing.

"Good morning, Karen. This is Santana Jackson. I'm here at my client's house, and I don't see my name on the schedule. I was just wondering what's going on?"

"Ah, yes… well, Santana. Mr. Davis called and asked for a new caregiver. He didn't say what happened or anything; he just asked for a new caregiver. I apologize for the misunderstanding. Since you showed up and didn't know, we're going to pay you for those hours you would've worked today. We can fill your Wednesday and Thursday for you, if you'd like?"

Hearing that *Mr. Davis* cancelled me as his caregiver, I was heated. Both JD and Juwelz were Mr. Davis. I knew exactly which Mr. Davis she was referring to.

"Um, no, ma'am. I'll leave both Wednesday and Thursday free. Thank you so much. Can you get me back on the phone with Courtney, please?" I politely asked. I had to apologize to her for how rudely I spoke to her. My mama taught me to always repent.

"Hello, this is Courtney." She came back on the line, just as cheerful.

"Hey, Courtney. This is Santana. I apologize for being so blunt earlier. I had no right. You didn't do anything wrong. Thank you so much for not getting an attitude back." I meant that sincerely. I shouldn't have been taking my attitude out on her. The person I needed to be taking it out on, I would do just that.

Look, Jesus, you're still working on me.

6

Juwelz

As usual, we were having a good day in the shop. Everyone was in a good mood, talking, clowning, and laughing. Right now, the joke was about Aaron's latest jump-off. He was telling us about his wild night with her.

"Y'all, I promise I never dealt with no mess like this! This girl was all over the place. Then her husband—"

"Husband!" Everyone in the shop exclaimed with surprise.

"Didn't I tell y'all she had a husband?"

"No!"

"Well, yeah, she got a husband and three kids—"

"Three kids! Damnnn!"

"Ju, this a judgement free zone, right?" Aaron asked with his arms opened to the space around him.

I nodded, making eye contact with him. "You know it is."

"Then why everybody judging for?" He spun around with his arms still out. The whole shop erupted into laughter once again.

"Man, we sorry, A. It's just this is funny. You never got with a married woman," I acknowledged. He'd been with older women. They were all single, from what he knew and told us.

"Yeah, man, or one with kids," Sean pointed out. I nodded in agreement.

Next, Cheyenne, the beautician, spoke up. "Right. They all be having big booties and be old biddies."

Everyone snickered at the mention of that. Aaron waved her and everybody else off. "Man, y'all telling me and I be there. But yeah, this was some other stuff. A brotha don't need them type of problems."

"Then a *brotha* need to stop doing what he's doing." Cyn laughed from behind the counter. Aaron's head snapped in her direction.

"Cyn, I swear I would change all my ways if you'd just give a brotha the time of day. You the type of woman that could settle any dog down."

"Not that dog, Cyn! Girl, he got fleas!" Cheyenne called out, causing the whole shop to erupt into laughter.

"Ohhh, that's cold!" The dude in Sean's chair instigated.

"For real," somebody else added.

"Aye, aye, aye. Y'all leave my dawg alone. He don't know no better… only what he was taught." I tried to help my brotha out.

"Yup, sounds like a dog to me!" Cyn sang out, followed by uncontrollable laughter.

I waved her off and swung my arm around A's shoulder. "Look, man—"

Ding!

"Saaan!" I heard Cyn sing after the door opened. I turned to see the woman I couldn't get off my brain for three days and two nights. San had left a bruise on my pride by turning me down on Sunday.

"Hey, Cyn!" San embraced Cyn with a smile. I was hating on the low. She acted like she didn't want to hug me on Sunday. You know those stiff hugs people give you?

"How are you, boo? Are you not working with my uncle anymore?" Cyn asked, her voice full of concern. She glanced up at me and back to San. San glared at me, burning a hole into my face. I stepped over to where they were standing.

"Hey, love. Is my dad okay?" Feeling the tightness in my stomach, I started to feel like I had to puke. This reminded me of the day I found out my mother was dying. I was sick to my stomach and had the runs that day.

"Hmm... I wouldn't know if your dad was okay, now would I?" San asked with a raised eyebrow. Cyn stood there looking confused in the face. I could tell she was trying figure out what San was talking about, as well as I.

"I don't know what you mean. San, why would you not know? Where is my dad? Is he alright?"

She scoffed, rolling her eyes. "Oh, please. Don't give me that mess. Don't stand there like you don't know what's going on, just 'cause you in front of your friends."

"San..." I felt myself getting upset as I inched closer to her. I wasn't with the type of games she was playing. This was my father's life she was talking about. "Where. Is. My. Father?"

"Ju-Ju..." Cyn reached up and touched my chest. I glanced at her and saw that she was shaking her head. "Calm down, bro."

"Not until she tells me what's going on with my dad!" I raised my voice, causing the entire shop to get quiet. At first, everyone was carrying on in their own conversations.

Now that they'd heard me talking loud, they'd stopped what they were doing.

"Okay, what is going on, y'all? This is too much. San, is there something wrong with my uncle?" Cyn got frustrated and asked. San shifted the little weight she carried to one leg and placed her hands on her hips.

"Why'd you do it, Juwelz? Huh?" she asked with much attitude.

"Why'd I'd do what, San? Huh?" I was now pretty much in her face. She didn't budge a muscle.

"Was it because I turned you down Sunday? Is that why you don't want me taking care of your dad anymore? You think that's going to get you a better chance? Huh? 'Cause it's not! To think I was going to give you a chance. I was going to come over today and tell you that I'd go out with you, despite the agency's rules! But, no. You had to go and mess with my money! My livelihood! My son's livelihood!"

"San—"

"No! I don't want to hear it, Ju! You can't lie your way out of this!" Her face was red, and her chest was rapidly, deeply moving up and down. She looked as if she was on the verge of tears.

"San... look, I have no idea what you're talking about. I don't have anything to do with you not taking care of my father anymore, okay?"

She lowly chuckled. It was almost crazy like. "They said... they said that *Mr. Davis* cancelled services with me. I already said you can't lie your way out of this, Ju." She glared at me with hatred in her eyes.

"Look, whatever *they* told you, it wasn't me... okay? Why would I cancel services with you? My father loves you! I can't believe you would even come into my shop accusing me of taking food out of you and your son's mouth! That's not me, San! I don't know what you been through and with who… but, that's not me!"

"If you didn't do it, then who did, Ju? Huh? Who!"

"I don't know!"

We were now toe to toe in a screaming match, with everybody in the shop watching. Was it ironic that in the back of my mind, I was praying that no one had their phones out recording this? I mean, they had almost every right since San and I were out in the open.

"Hey! Stop it!" Cyn yelled over our yelling. "Enough!"

"But he started it!"

"She's crazy!"

"I said enough!" Cyn's chest was now heaving up and down. She was out of breath. "San… this is all just one big misunderstanding."

"Misunderstanding? No, Cyn, this is more like a man can't have what he wants, so he throws a tantrum by *handling it the way he sees fit*!" San was talking to Cyn but looking directly at me.

"I keep telling you that it wasn't me!" I defended myself.

"I don't believe you!"

"I don't care! That's my word, and I'm sticking to it!"

"It was Uncle!" Cyn yelled, causing us both to snap our mouths shut.

"What!" we exclaimed in unison. Cyn nodded.

"I called him while y'all was screaming each other's head off. He said that he asked for a new caregiver. It was nothing against San. In fact, he loves San like the daughter he wished he had."

After Cyn revealed that, I didn't know what to say. San stood there looking like she was in a daze. I could tell she was searching for the words to say, just like I was.

"Juwelz, I'm—"

"Get out," I calmly commanded.

"What?" I heard San's voice crack.

"Get out." I repeated myself in an even tone before completely walking away. "And everybody, get back to work!"

Lord... I tried.

7

Santana

Two weeks later...

"Mommy, does it look I need my hair cut again? Look, it's growing back, and I want Juwelz to cut it again. He cut good!"

This was the first thing that came out of Leek's mouth when he got into the car. No hey mommy, I love you, I miss you or how was your day. Just straight to getting his hair cut by Juwelz.

Biting my bottom lip, I contemplated on how I would tell him that wasn't happening. Before I could do so, Leek said, "Plus, Mommy, he said to come back in two weeks. It's been two weeks. I counted and everything."

Since when did this boy care about his hair being cut? No, since when did it matter *who* cut it? "Umm, baby, I don't know."

"But whyyy?" Leek whined.

How could I tell my baby that his mama ruined his chances at ever getting his hair cut by Juwelz again? That I went up to that shop and acted a fool, when really, I had no right? That I wanted so badly to apologize to Ju, but I knew he didn't want anything to do with me anymore? I hadn't even seen him at church in the last two weeks.

"I think Juwelz is busy, baby. How about we find you a different barber?" I tried to sweet talk him. He folded his arms and puffed out his chest.

"No," he simply replied. Ugh, he was so much like his dad in some ways. Leek probably would never know, but he was. Like his stubbornness for one. Isaac was so stubborn when we were together. I thought I could get away from him somehow. Yet here he was, showing himself in my son.

"Leek, we're not doing this. I said no, and that's final."

"But, Mamaaa!" he exaggerated.

"Boy, 'but, mama' me one more time and see what happens!"

"But—"

"Leek! I said no!" I popped his exposed thigh. He was wearing a light gray and red Nike short set with shoes to match today.

I wasn't surprised when he didn't cry. Leek hardly ever cried when I popped him anymore. He just got an attitude. That was okay, because we were going to the store. We'd see who had the attitude when we got there.

It was just like I thought. As soon as we pulled into Safeway's parking lot, he was asking for some candy. As bad as I wanted to say, *naw, homie, keep that same energy*, I also couldn't tell him no, knowing good and well this boy was going to walk out with something anyways.

I was busy putting some bananas and grapes in the basket when I heard a familiar deep voice talking to Malik. Glancing in their direction, I noticed it was Juwelz.

Way to talk him up, Leek. I rolled my eyes to the ceiling. *Okay, San... just be cool. Be polite and move along.* Yes, I was telling myself this as I walked over to Leek and Ju. The

42

closer I got, the more nervous I was becoming. I wanted to turn around and go hide in another aisle. Ugh, why was I acting like a high school girl who was afraid of her crush?

"Juwelz, oh, hi! I thought that was you. I couldn't tell, but now I know!" *San, what the heck was that? You know you saw that man!*

Juwelz didn't even look my way. He continued to have his conversation with Leek. "Aight, little man… Let your mama know, and I'll see you tomorrow." After he said that, he pushed his cart off in the opposite direction.

Did that just happen? Did he just completely ignore me like I wasn't standing here? No. Did he just have my son give me a message and I was standing here? "What the…"

"Mama!" Leek tried to get my attention. I was still looking in the direction Juwelz had gone in. I so badly wanted to go after him and run him over with my cart. *Okay, San, quit being petty.*

"Mama!" Leek tugged on the back of my shirt.

"Huh?" Shaking my head, I focused on my son. He had an innocent expression on his face.

"Juwelz said I could come and get my hair cut tomorrow, after school. He said only if you say it's okay though." Given the expression on Leek's face, I didn't want to tell him no. Given the way Juwelz had me feeling right now… I wanted to say hell no!

"Can I please, Mama? Please?" He got my attention, bringing it back to his question.

Sighing in defeat, I thought… *how could I tell a face so cute no?* "Okay, Malik… You can get your hair cut by Juwelz tomorrow."

"Yaaay! Thanks, Mama! I really like Ju. He's cool, and he likes basketball. He said I could come and watch the game this season at the shop. Can I, Mama? Can I, please?" Leek jumped up and down as we moved through the store.

"Malik, calm down, and I'll think about it. Okay?" I didn't mean to sound so irritate with him. I was just in my feelings.

"Okay... oh! Here is his number. He said to call him to set up the appointment." Leek pulled a piece of paper out his pants pocket and passed it to me.

~&~

Two hours. It'd been two hours since we had gotten home from the store. I had dinner going while Malik was at the table doing his homework. We were having baked chicken, homemade mashed potatoes with gravy, and mixed veggies. I wanted to have something simple but balanced. When I used to work at the facility, I would always pop something like those processed chicken nuggets into the oven. Now that I had more time on my hands, I was able to cook actual meals.

Come on and just call this man and make the appointment, I told myself as I sat on the couch looking at the piece of paper with Juwelz's number on it. I'd been thinking about what I'd say when I called Juwelz for the past two hours. I only had to make an appointment, but I wanted to say more. I needed to say more. I needed to apologize for my behavior. That was the only way to get this feeling of guilt off my conscience. If he didn't want to talk to me after that, I'd be cool. I'd just continue to live my life like I didn't ever meet a Juwelz Davis.

"Hello." His deep voice came booming from the other end of the receiver. Instantly, I froze up and forgot what I was going to say. "Hello? Is anybody there?"

"Hello... hey, Juwelz. Malik gave me your number to

44

call and confirm his appointment for tomorrow at three thirty?" I quickly got out.

"Yeah, I did," he simply replied.

"Okay. I'll bring him at that time then."

"Alright then. Was that it?"

"Um… actually… I wanted to apologize to you for how I acted that day at your shop. It was wrong of me to accuse you of something you didn't do. I was just upset, and my vision was clouded." There. I said what I needed to say.

"It's all good, love. Don't beat yourself up about it, okay? Look, I got dinner going, so I got to go. See you tomorrow."

"Okay, have a—"

Click!

That was it. He hung up the phone before I could say anything else. Oh well… at least I apologized. But I had a feeling that wasn't enough. I may've truly messed up with him.

Jesus, fix it!

8

Juwelz

Ding!

Hearing the door open, I shot from my chair to see who had walked in. It wasn't who I wanted and hoped to be. It was just Cyn coming back inside from her break. I thought it was Santana and Malik. I peeked up at the clock and noticed it wasn't quite time yet.

Three thirty couldn't get here fast enough. I couldn't wait to see San's beautiful face walk through the door. I knew I acted like an a-hole to her last night. The truth was, I wasn't even upset with her anymore. I couldn't say why I acted like that, because I didn't know myself. I prayed she would talk to me when she came in today with Malik. The way I acted on the phone last night, I wanted to apologize. In fact, my dad was counting on it. He had overheard the way I spoke to her and got on me about it. I promised him I'd smooth things over with San. Not only for him, but for me.

I also got a clean confession out of him. I went home that day San went off on me and was livid with my father. He explained why he cancelled her services, and it made sense to me. He said that in some ways, she reminded him of my mother. The way San cared for him those two days made him think his wife was around. He felt it was wrong to have her there and he was thinking of my mother, so he called and asked for somebody new. Yes, he loved San, but it saddened him when she would come and then have to leave. He also told me he let her go because he recognized the way I stared at her. He said there was a twinkle in my eye. Now that part, I couldn't deny if I wanted to.

"Man, you been staring at that clock for a little while now. Either you got a client coming in, or you waiting on a call. What is it?" Aaron pointed out as he walked back over to his station. He'd just come from the back.

"Honestly, man?" I spun my chair around to face him.

He nodded with a somber expression. "Honestly."

"I'm waiting for San to get here with Malik. They're supposed to be coming at three thirty." I let go of the deep breath I was holding. I was never one to hide my feelings. So telling A that I basically had feelings for San was no big thing to me. He liked to clown on the fellas when he heard we wanted more out of life than what we had. I knew me, for sure. I wanted a wife and some kids of my own. I wouldn't mind San being my wife and her having my kids.

"San... San... San..." He looked to the ceiling. I assumed he was jogging his memory. "San! Ohhh! You mean that crazy lady who came up in here and went off on you?"

I hung my head and shook it. I couldn't lie. I was also nervous for San to come in today. I wasn't 100 percent sure that everyone had forgot about her last visit. "Man... don't hold that against her. She was having a bad day."

"I know you not defending that type of crazy... man. Baby girl need a check if she acting like that. Ju, you my bro, and I love you. You deserve—"

Ding!

Thank God. Saved by the bell, I thought as my head shot in that direction. "Juwelz!"

I noticed Malik running in but not San. "Hey, little man. Where is your mama?"

"She's—"

"Little boy, what did I tell you about running?" I recognized the woman I knew as Mother Jackson that went to my church. "Oh, hey, Julius. How are you?"

I heard her question, but I was too busy staring past her head to see if her daughter was going to walk in next. "Julius?"

"Oh, I'm sorry, Ms. Jackson—"

"I am for real! Never meant to make your daughter cry. I apologize a... too soon?" This fool Aaron, man. I cracked a smirk but waved him off.

"I'm sorry about that, Ms. Jackson. I'm doing good. How are you? Would you like some water, coffee, or tea?" I took her by the hand and led her to the seating area. She didn't necessarily need any help getting there, but it was in me to help her. It was just the way I was raised.

"Yes, some coffee would be fine. Three creams and three sugars, please," she politely asserted.

"Yes, ma'am. Coming right up." I stood to go do that for her, and she stopped me by grabbing my hand. "Julius, I know all about what happened here with you and my daughter. I know she's apologized, but I'd like to do so as well. Santana wasn't raised to disrupt peace like that, no matter how upset she was. I hope you'll find it in your heart to forgive her. She would've come here with Leek today, but she was too embarrassed. Okay, baby, I just thought you should know that."

"Thank you for telling me that, Ms. Jackson. I accept you all's apology. I'll get that coffee for you now." Walking toward the back, I felt at peace now. I just hoped San was alright.

~&~

After a long day at the shop, I didn't even feel like coming home and cooking. I stopped by our new favorite Chinese spot, Cathy's, and ordered a family meal. When I got in the house, I caught the new caregiver, Mindy, asleep on the couch. My father was sitting in his usual spot, watching *Family Feud*.

"What's up, Pops?" I asked loud enough to make my presence known to Mindy. She quickly shot up from her spot on the couch and glanced around like she was spooked. "Hello, Mindy. You having a nice nap?"

"Oh, Mr. Davis. I'm sorry for falling asleep. Please don't tell on me. I just got this job, and I'm in school, and—"

"Mindy, Mindy, Mindy!" I had to raise my voice to get her attention. "Calm down. I'm not upset you fell asleep. Trust me, I know what you going through. I remember being in college, and it's hard." I also peeped her biology books and binder stacked up on the table.

"It might be hard, but it's worth it, right?" She weakly smiled. Seeing the rings around her eyes, I felt for baby girl.

"Yeah, it's worth it. Hey, Mindy, I got my dad tonight. You head home and get some rest."

"Are you sure, Mr. Davis?" she sheepishly questioned. I nodded.

"Yeah, I'm sure, Mindy. Go ahead and go home."

"Thank you so much, Mr. Davis." She packed her stuff up and prepared to head out. Having someone younger call me Mr. Davis was a little odd. I mean, I was twenty-seven, not some old man.

"Hey, Mindy. You can call me Julius or Juwelz."

"Okay, Mr—Julius! See you tomorrow, JD!"

"See ya!" my father and I answered in unison.

"Alright, Pops. Let's eat!" I came out the kitchen to set the plates down and almost dropped them. For the first time in a long time, my father was using his cane to walk to the dining room. He usually used his wheelchair.

"Oh boy, don't have a heart attack," he joked as he came and sat down. This man up and walking around wasn't my father. Well, he used to be, but when he got sick, I thought he was slowly deteriorating. To see him up and walking around now had me in my feelings.

"Wow, Dad… you're walking—were walking." I set his plate in front of him and took my seat.

"Yeah, son. I surprised myself. When San was here, she helped me—"

"Wait… San?" I set my fork down.

"Yeah, San helped me. She showed me how to use my cane."

"Pops, you know how many times I tried to get you to use your cane?"

"Yeah, son, I know, but then I didn't want to use it. I didn't want to appear helpless, so I refused. After I had that last flare up, I ended up in the chair. I took it as God punishing me for not trying to use the cane because the chair was more humiliating than the cane," he revealed. "Honestly, son, I didn't think I'd ever use that cane. But when San came, she asked me why I didn't use it. After I told her, she convinced me to try. I did, and now look at me. I'm back in business, baby," he joked. "Ahh, that San is something special. Why did I cancel her again?"

I side-eyed him with a knowing look. "You know why

you cancelled her, Pops. Remember? She reminded you of Mom?"

He nodded with a solemn expression. "Yeah, true. But that's not the only reason, son."

"What other reason could there be?"

"You, son," he revealed.

"Me?"

"Yeah, I saw the way you looked at her. You want that woman. You can't have her if she working here. For one, it's against the agency's policy." I laughed at him saying the same thing San had said.

"Yeah, that's what San said." Scooping some rice into my mouth, I asked, "You said for one. What's the second reason?"

"Oh! For two, I wasn't about to share a girl with you. You got to get your own, son!" he joked. All I could do was laugh at him. Man, my dad was something else.

Thank you, Lord, for sending Santana our way.

9

Santana

"Wakanda forevereeerr!" Leek danced around the living room in his Black Panther pajamas, chanting.

It was Friday night, so we were going to watch movies on Netflix and eat snacks all night. I almost missed it, until Leek pointed out that *Black Panther* was on here. Now we were about to watch it.

"Ma, watch this!" Leek was on the floor, in a position to do a handstand.

"Leek, chill out, baby. Come have a seat before you hurt yourself," I warned in a syrupy tone. I always gave him the first warning in a nice and calm tone. It was when I had to tell him more than once that I'd start going off and yelling at him.

I was satisfied and a bit surprised that he listened the first time. He usually went ahead and did what he was going to do and suffered through me yelling at him.

"Oh, Mama! Can I call Juwelz? I want to make an appointment," Leek asked in a serious tone.

I gave him the side eye. "Excuse me, sir? You just got

your hair cut. You'll see him again in another month." That was usually the amount of time it took to grow back.

"Juwelz said that I should keep it cut every two weeks. I got to look good for the ladies." He nodded his head with a Kool-Aid smile stretching across his face.

"The ladies? What ladies!" I thought I was having a mini heart attack.

My baby was only eight. What he knew about *the ladies*? I bet Juwelz and his friends were talking about that today in his shop. See, it was one thing for Malik to go get his hair cut. If he was going to be coming home talking about *the ladies*, he wasn't going back to that shop!

"Oh, nuh uhn. Let me call Ju—"

"Mama, chill on my bro. Aaron is the one who told me I got to stay looking right for the ladies, not Juwelz," Leek informed me. I was now staring at this boy like had just sprouted a second head right before my eyes. Who was this boy, and what did he do with my son?

"Okay, and who is Aaron? See, I knew I should've gone ahead to the shop with you." Ugh, it served me right for being scary.

It'd been two weeks since everything went down. I was still scared and somewhat embarrassed about the way I acted. That was the reason I sent my mom to go with Leek. She obviously wasn't paying attention to the conversation at hand, because my son had a new attitude.

"You know what, never mind. I'll call and ask Juwelz myself." Yes. I was being that kind of mom right now. Leek gasped like I was being annoying. See, nuh uhn. "I'll be right back, Leek. Here, watch the movie."

"*Mamaaa…*"

"Nuh uhn, I don't want to hear it." I got up and went to the back where my room was. As soon as I sat down to call Ju, my phone began to vibrate in my palm. He was calling *me*!

Come on, San. Answer the phone! "Okay, ugh… hello?" I tried to answer like I wasn't excited that he was calling me, when really, I was.

"Hey, love. I know it's late, but I wanted to call and check on you and Leek," he smoothly revealed.

"Aww, okay. Yeah, I was just thinking about you too." *Darn it, San! Noo, don't tell him that!* I was kicking myself for revealing that part.

"Oh yeah. What were you thinking?" I could hear that ugly smirk all in voice. Ugh, that ugly but sexy smirk he wore whenever I saw him. That smirk that I sometimes saw when I closed my eyes before I fell asleep at night. That smirk that I wanted to slap right off his face. That smirk that I wanted to just… kiss! Lawd, that smirk!

"Malik was telling me that you said he should get his hair cut every two weeks. He also told me that someone in your shop by the name of Aaron told him he needed to look fresh for the ladies? Juwelz, if this is the kind of stuff that's happening in your shop, I can't let my son get his hair cut there anymore. I don't need those type of thoughts to be embedded in his young mind. Getting women should be the last thing on his mind. All Malik should be thinking about right now is doing good in school and being a kid." I was out of breath after getting all of that out. I was happy that Ju didn't cut me off or try to over talk me though. He actually listened to me, waiting for me to finish.

"Is that it, love?" There went that stupid smirk again.

I didn't know whether to get smart or to remain calm and ignore his question. In actuality, I wanted to do both, if that made any sense. "Um, yeah… I guess."

"Okay, love. Well, first, I got on Aaron about those things he told Malik. Aaron knows I don't condone certain things in the shop—especially, when there is a child present. He got a little carried away. It was handled, love—"

"Okay, bu—"

"Hey, love. Did I not let you speak?"

"You did." I rolled my eyes.

"Did I not ask you was that it?" he continued his interrogation.

"You did." I rolled my eyes again.

"Aight then. Now like I was saying... the situation was handled. Okay?" I nodded, even though he couldn't see me. "Hello?"

"Uh, yeah, I'm still here. Thank you for cutting his hair anyways. I truly appreciate it." I had softened my tone. I was learning and taking heed to certain things about Ju. Like, how you came at him, he gave you the same energy.

"It was no problem. Malik is a special kid," he complimented. That made me smile so hard. I was blushing all on the other line. If Juwelz could see me now.

"Thank you so much."

"You're very welcome. How are you though? I missed your face today. Why didn't you come?" he inquired.

"Um..." I didn't quite know what to say. I could easily lie and say that I had work. That wasn't true. It was more like I was too afraid and ashamed to show my face at his shop. "I uh... I didn't know if I was welcomed."

"Why wouldn't you be welcomed, San?" See, now I knew he was trying to play. I could hear the amusement in his voice.

"Ju... I'm not about to do this with you tonight. You know why! You kicked me out, remember?"

"Did I?" he joked.

"Bye, Ju—"

"San, San, San. I'm just playing, baby girl." He

cracked up. Lawd, this man was so intoxicating. His laugh, smile, and ugh... just him was everything. "But I want you to know that you're always welcome at the shop. That day was rough, yeah, but it's all good."

Exhaling, I was able to breathe better. "Thank you, Ju... and again, I apologize for how I came at you. I just wish I knew why JD didn't want me around anymore. I thought we were cool. I know it was only a couple of days, but he grew on me... you know?"

"Yeah, I know. He kind of has that impression on everyone that comes across him." Ju lightly chuckled.

"Could you tell me why he can—"

"Go to dinner with me." He said it so fast, I needed him to repeat himself to make sure I heard him right.

"Huh?"

"Go to dinner with me, San," he repeated in a clear and firm tone. It wasn't forceful but gentle and clear. Dang it. I couldn't tell this man no again. He obviously wanted my time if this was his third time asking.

"Um, I don't know, Juwelz." I shook my head. I was having all types of doubts running through my mind.

"Come on, San. What do you have to lose?" He sounded so convincing. Still, I had doubts. I hadn't dated or even been intimate with a human being since Isaac. Lord knew, that was eight years ago.

"What do you mean, what do I have to lose? I have a lot going on in my life, Juwelz. I come with a lot. I don't know—"

"San?" He got my attention, stopping me from rambling off my excuses.

"Huh?"

"It's just dinner between two friends, love." He sounded amused. I bet he had that stupid smirk on his face

56

too. Once again, Ju had managed to make me feel embarrassed.

"Okay, fine, but I'm paying for myself. That way you know this isn't a date. Got it?" I tried to bargain with him. For a second the line went dead. Suddenly, I heard his deep voice gargling with laughter.

"Damn, woman. You ain't having it, huh?"

"Not at all." I giggled. I probably sounded crazy to him, but oh well. This was who I was. I didn't only have myself to think about. I had a son. I had to think clear and make the right decisions for him.

"You can bring Malik if you'd like." He surprised me when he said that.

"Hmm… Okay, I think I will." Having Malik there would make it seem less like a date and more like an outing between friends.

"How about Dave & Buster's on Saturday?" he suggested. I wasn't going to lie. I just got a little excited for myself. I hadn't been there in a while. Well, I hadn't let loose and just had some fun in a while. With work, school, and Malik, I was busy. I was happy to be on somewhat of a break from school now. I still had one more year left before I was an RN.

"Okay, sounds like fun!"

"Okay, cool." He yawned into the receiver, causing goosebumps to prickle my arms, legs, and back.

"Okay…"

"Good night, San."

"Oh! Yeah, good night." I shook my head, getting my head out of the clouds. I couldn't help it. Juwelz was fine. Him being respectable only added to his perfect persona.

Thank you, Lord, for sending Juwelz our way…

10

Juwelz

You ever get nervous and don't know why? It's just a feeling that creeps up on you and you can't shake it, no matter how hard you try? Then what makes it worse, you don't know if it's for a good reason or a bad one? That was exactly how I was feeling, waiting for San and Leek to show up at Dave & Buster's.

I had already got us a table, so it wouldn't be an issue when they got here. That way we could just order food and go play some games.

While I was waiting, I checked my messages and social media notifications. There were a few people on Instagram liking and commenting on my pics of some of the cuts I did. Those same people were in my DM's inquiring about when I could get them or their kids in my chair. After getting that squared away, I shot Cyn a text message. She was at the house with my dad until I got back. I could've called *Visiting Angels* to send a care-giver, but Cyn was more than happy to chill with her uncle.

Me: *Y'all good? Need anything?*

Cyn: *We good over here. Shouldn't you be focusing on your date with San?*

Me: *It's not a date, big head girl. I told you that though.*

Cyn: *Right, because everybody worries about how they look when they just going to Dave&Buster's.*

I shook my head, laughing at her text. She was right though. I asked her several times if what I had on was too casual. It'd been a while since I'd been out on a date with a woman. San could say this wasn't a date. Yet, why did it feel like one? I invited Malik to make her feel more comfortable. I also picked this place so that he would have something to do. It offered benefits for all of us. San and I could talk and get to know each other better, while Malik went bananas on arcade games.

Me: *Whatever man. I'll see you later. Don't burn my house down trying to cook. LOL!*

Cyn: *Whatever! I know how to cook!*

I didn't even bother responding as I laughed at her last text. Of course Cyn could cook, but I loved to tease her as if she didn't. Being our parents only children, Cyn and I treated each other more like siblings.

"Ahem." I heard someone clearing their throat from behind me and turned to see San standing, holding Malik's hand.

"Ju!" Malik exclaimed and ran over to me and gave me a hug around my waist. I hugged him back with my arm around his shoulders.

"Aye, what's good, lil' man?"

"You sure are grinning all in your phone. Who is she?" San slowly walked up, asking with a grin on her face.

"Huh?" I looked at her sideways.

"I seen you smiling, all in your phone from the door. I was wondering who was the special lady that had you showing all thirty-twos?" She shifted her stance with one hand on her hip. Though she had a smile on her face, her tone told a different story. It was one of those warning tones your mother gave you when you were doing something wrong.

"Oh, that was Cyn, love." I lightly laughed.

"Ohhh, hmm. How is Cyn doing? I need to come by the shop and see her." San came over and took a seat in the booth, across from me.

"I can ask her if you can have her number, if you want?"

"Yes, I would love that!" San cheerfully exclaimed.

I pulled my phone out and shot Cyn a text and slipped it back into my jeans pocket. "What's up, little man? You ready to play some games?"

"Yeah!" He jumped up and down.

"Aight, lil' man. Let's go get these game cards." I got up and took Malik by the hand. Before we fully walked away, I turned to look at San. She had this look on her face that I couldn't make out. "You good, love? You need anything?"

She gave me a toothy smile. "Yeah, I'm good, boo. I don't need anything right now."

"Okay then. You can order the food while we get the cards."

"Cool," she simply replied with a shrug.

Once we were at a distance from San, Malik pointed something out to me. "Ju, don't get mad, but I think my mom likes you."

I couldn't help but laugh. Kids, man, I swear. They're bolder these days than when I was a kid his age. "How you figure that, man? And why would I get upset? I like your mom too."

"You do?" Malik's eyes lit up, and a smile spread across his face.

I nodded to him. "Yeah, I do. So what makes you think she likes me?"

"It's like what Aaron said. You know when a girl likes you when she rolls her eyes at you, or she's mean to you."

"Your mama mean to me and rolls her eyes at me?" I played along.

"Yeah, I heard the way she talked to you. She rolls her eyes around you a lot too. Sooo, that means she likes you." Leek giggled at the end.

Man, when a kid noticed stuff you thought only grown people did, there was a problem. Me and San obviously had to watch ourselves, how we acted and talked to one another around Leek. He clearly was a smart kid and picked up on our vibes. Well, that and A was running his mouth to him. I was just as pissed that Aaron was telling Leek about girls as San was. I had a feeling I wouldn't hear the last of it. The woman clearly didn't play about her son, as she shouldn't. If I let him, A would mess my chances with her up before I could steal the first kiss.

"Aye, lil' man. I got to ask you a serious question." I got down on one knee, looking him in the eyes. I could tell he knew this was truly serious because he stopped moving and got focused. "How do you feel about me dating your mom?"

I know it might be weird to some that I'm asking this eight-year-old kid to date his mom. The truth of the matter, Leek was all San had. He was literally the only man she was obligated to have in her life. To have another man, a man that wanted to pursue her step in, was going to take a toll on both her and Malik.

"You mean like take her out to nice places and make her smile?" Leek questioned in a serious tone.

I nodded my head with a smile. "Yeah, little man. That's exactly what I want to do."

"I'm cool with that. She needs to get out and smile more anyways." He quickly threw his shoulders into a shrug.

Shaking my head, I just laughed. *Thank you again, God.*

"What took y'all so long to come back?" San asked as soon as we got back to the table.

"We were waiting in line. There was a family ahead of us," I answered.

"Oh, okay. Well I ordered wings, sliders, and fries. I hope that's okay." She half smiled. I rubbed my stomach, thinking about how good the food would be going into my system. I don't remember the last I ate today, and my ribs were touching my back.

"That's cool with me." I looked at Leek and he nodded.

He was too busy glancing around, trying to figure out what he was going to play first. Little man was talking my ear off in the line about all the games he couldn't wait to play. I didn't mind. I was glad to listen to him talk. Most kids, especially boys, didn't care to talk to a man that was interested in their mom.

After an hour went by, I was starting to get tired. I swear I'd been on every game at least three times with Leek. He was having fun, so that was what mattered to me. A few times I caught San watching us with a smile on her face like a creep.

"Come on, Juuu! We can play the car game again. This time I'm going to kick your butt!" Leek gloated. He was sitting on the inside, eating fries, on my side of the booth.

Me and San sat eating and laughing with him. I was actually surprised she didn't order a salad. That's what chicks did at places like this. I had remembered that Santana Jackson wasn't like any other woman I met.

"I'm ready to go. Come on, Ju!" Leek was nudging me to get up.

"Leek, baby, wait a minute. Let Ju rest, baby," San spoke in a sweet tone. I looked over at Leek, and he nodded.

"Well can I go play more games? I'll wait for you to play the car game with me, Ju, okay?"

"Aight, lil' man. I got you." I moved out his way.

As he took off running, San called after him. "Walk, Leek!"

"Man, he has so much energy. For a minute, I forgot I was twenty-one years older than him. After about the third round of games, I was spent. I must be out of shape." I rubbed my belly, which was growling again. I had just finished the last slider on my plate. I noticed there were two wings and a slider left.

"You want this last slider?" I offered to San. She smiled at me and slowly shook her head no.

"I'm good. I haven't even finished what's on my plate yet. Thank you for asking though."

"Of course, love. You enjoying yourself?"

"I actually am. I haven't had fun like this in a long time. Thank you so much, Ju. I want to thank you for inviting Leek too. He needed this as much as I did."

"No problem, love. I'd like to do this again…with me and you."

"Ju…" She shook her head with a smile. "I already told you that I wasn't trying to be nothing but friends."

"Okay, so friends can't go out and see a movie together?"

"Lawd… huuuh!" She giggled, making my heart skip a beat. I loved the way this woman smiled. It was everything. Her laugh was like medicine to my soul. "What movie you want to go see, friend?"

"What's your favorite throwback movie?" I wondered.

"Um... hmm... *Brown Sugar*," she answered before taking a bite out of her fry.

"Hmm... okay." I nodded, already making up a plan.

"What about yours?" She shocked me with that question.

"*The Wood*."

"Aww! That's my second favorite. I haven't seen it in so long. I might go home and watch it," she teased.

"Now I know you not up here telling me that and not inviting your *friend* to come and watch with you."

"I mean... you can if you want. We could watch *Brown Sugar*, too," she offered.

"Then what are we going to do on our date?" I smirked. She rolled her eyes and grinned.

"See, here go you. I swear you pushing it. We not dating, Ju." She laughed.

"Aight, well if we watch both movies tonight, what are we going to do next weekend?"

"I'm sure you'll figure it out."

"I'm sure I will. What do you like to eat?"

"I love spaghetti with fried chicken and cornbread on the side. It was my favorite meal my mama cooked, growing up."

"That sounds good right about now."

"It does! Mmm, see now I'm going to have to stop at the store and get the stuff for dinner tonight." She gushed. To see the excitement on her face made smile. I could sit and stare at San's beautiful self all day.

"So not only did you invite me over to watch our favorite movies, you also inviting me over to have dinner? This date is going to be better than I thought it would."

"Boooyyaa! Bye! I'm not going to tell you again. This.

Is. Not. A. Date!" She was laughing, but I knew she was serious.

"What if we save all that for next weekend? You bring the spaghetti and a green salad. I'll fry some chicken and make the cornbread. I have *The Wood* and *Brown Sugar*. We can chill at your house or mine. It's up to you." I gave her ultimatums. As she stared off into space, I could see that she was really thinking about it.

"Okay. You come to my place with the movies, salad, and chicken. I'll cook the spaghetti and cornbread." She nodded with a smile, gazing at me. "Remember, this isn't a date. We just two buddies having dinner and watching movies. You got that?"

"I'm going to keep it real with you, San. I'm feeling you, and I want to get to know you better. I know you keep saying you not looking for nothing. With me, that's not the case. I'm looking and I'm going to find. This may not be anything to you." I moved my arms around for emphasis. "But I can't help but to see it as us moving in the direction that God wants us to be... together."

"Ju—" Usually, I didn't like cutting San off from talking. I wanted her to hear me and understand though.

"You don't have to respond now, San. Just give me a chance to show you that I can love you in every kind of way."

I watched her mouth drop into an O as she gasped. It was like a deep exhale. The way she was opening and closing her mouth, I thought she might say something. Instead of using her mouth to respond, she nodded her head.

Please, Lord, save her for me. Do this one favor for me...

11

Santana

Just give me a chance to show you that I can love you in every kind of way... Juwelz's words had been playing in my head like a broken record all week. No matter how hard I tried, I couldn't get this man's words out my head. I actually wanted to hear him say it again, like I craved it. I *needed* his words. They did something to me, made me think and wish for us a future together.

It wasn't that I didn't necessarily want one. I was just guarded because I'd been hurt before. It happened so long ago, but I didn't want to feel that pain again.

"Mommy, don't forget to save me some spaghetti!" Leek sounded like somebody's man from the living room. He was in there playing his PlayStation 4. He'd been begging me to get him 2k19 all week, since it just came out.

"Boy, I know you better turn your voice down," I gave fair warning.

"Sorry, ma'am! Can you please save me some spaghetti?"

"Yes, I will. You got your bags together?"

"Yes, ma'am. What time is Grandma getting here because I'm trying to get a couple more games in before she comes."

"Um, she should be here in an hour. I'm going to call her in a minute."

Knock! Knock!

"She's here? Aww man!" Malik huffed out, throwing a tantrum.

"Boy, I know you not mad about my—Juwelz? You're here early." I was surprised to see him standing there. In his hands he carried a pan with aluminum foil covering it and a bowl with plastic wrap.

"Really? I thought you said six." He smirked. Ugh, here we go.

"No, I said seven."

"You want me to come back at seven then?"

"No, come in. Here, I'll put this away. The spaghetti is in the oven now, and I was just about to mix your corn-bread and pop it in next." I took the dishes from him and moved out the way for him to come inside.

"Okay, that's cool."

"Ju!" I heard Malik exclaim from the kitchen. Our apartment wasn't super big, so the distance wasn't too far. I was able to look directly into the living area from my medium/small kitchen.

"What's up, lil' man? Aww, what you playing? Fortnite?" He took a seat on the couch. Malik was up and hooking his other game controller into the game. I got a tickle out of it. My baby was too happy to share his game with Juwelz.

"No. Mama won't let me play Fortnite. She said I'm too young," Leek sadly replied. I knew exactly what he was trying to do. He was trying to get Ju on his side so they could gang up on me. It had happened a few times during the week. Ju and I were on FaceTime, and Leek would ask me for something. I'd tell him no or that he had to wait until a certain time. He'd get Ju in and they'd double team me, making me give in.

"Well, your mama—"

"Ahem!" I cleared my throat, making my presence known, even though they knew I was standing right in the kitchen.

"Is a smart woman." Juwelz's laughter filled up the entire front room.

"Mhm!" I playfully rolled my eyes. I was checking the oven to see how the spaghetti looked and popping the cornbread in. "Ju?"

"Yes, my love?" he answered. In the knick of time, he'd gone from calling me love to *his love*. Every time he said it, my skin sprouted goosebumps and I felt butterflies churn in my stomach. Sometimes I called his name just to hear him say, *yes, my love?*

"Did you bring the movies? I didn't see them in your hands when I took the food."

"Oh, yeah, they right here." He pointed to them on the table.

"Okay, the spaghetti and cornbread will be done soon."

"Okay," Leek and Ju answered simultaneously.

Fifteen minutes later, the food was all done. Leek and Ju were all into their game as I fixed our plates. I couldn't help the smile that adorned my face or the content feeling I got having us all here. It was like it was meant to be.

"You need help with the plates, my love?" I didn't even feel Ju creep up behind me. I must've been too into my thoughts.

"Naw, boo. I got it. Go have a seat at the table… Leek, baby, go wash your hands and come sit at the table to eat."

"Okay, Mommy!" He paused his game and went to do what I'd told him.

My eyebrows shot up as I watched him. Okay, so either Malik was trying to impress Juwelz, or he was turning over a new leaf. This boy never just came when I told him to. He'd always had to play one more round of whatever game he was playing.

All during dinner, I watched and listened to Malik and Juwelz talk amongst each other. It was as if I wasn't even in the room. I took special notice to the glimmer in Malik's eye. It was one I never noticed before. Then it hit me. Ju was the first man that I ever let into our lives. My son was craving a male figure in his life.

"San, you good?" Ju touched my hand, snapping me from my thoughts.

"Yeah, I'm good. I spaced out for a minute."

"I see that. That's why I asked if you were good."

"Thank you." I moved my hand on top of his. He took it and gave it a gentle squeeze. Lord, that squeeze awoke not only my emotions but my southern center. *Jesus, be a fence all around me!* "This chicken, ahem… is really good."

Ju let my hand go and picked up his fork. "Yeah, this cornbread is on point too. Actually, it all tastes good. You not so bad in the kitchen."

"Oh boy, here go you." I cracked up. "You so full of yourself!"

"Confidence, baby, confidence."

"*Confidence!*" I mocked him, causing a laugh to come out of Leek and Ju.

Juwelz and I continued to go back and forth until there was a knock at the door. I knew it was only my mom. Truthfully, I forgot she was coming to get Malik.

"Hey, Mommy!" I clung to her like I always did. "You want a plate of food? We got spaghetti, chicken, salad, and cornbread." I was fast talking her to keep her attention on me. In my head, if I did this, it would help avoid the elephant in the room. It wasn't working though.

"Good evening, Mama Jackson," the elephant spoke.

"Julius! Aww, hi baby! *What a surprise!*" she emphasized. At the same time, she turned to look at me with raised eyebrows. I waited until she turned her head back toward him before I rolled my eyes. I wouldn't dare let her see me rolling my eyes and it was directed toward her? My mother was a strong believer in, *you ain't too old to get beat down.*

"I'll get Leek's things so y'all can go." I headed to his room with my mother following closely behind.

"Mhm!" She cleared her throat as she shut the door. A smile creeped up on my face. I already knew what this woman wanted.

"Nothing is going on between us, Ma. We just friends, I promise." I put my right hand up to the heavens.

"Friends with benefits?" she joked.

"What you know about friends with benefits, lady?"

"Honey, please! Ya mama ain't been saved all her life. I've had my share of special friends."

"Oh Lord, lady. I'm not hearing this." I shook my head, laughing. For as long as I knew, my mother had been saved, sanctified, and Holy Ghost filled. I didn't know the poor sick sinner her. So you could imagine me finding it hard to believe she had any *special friends.*

"Whatever. It's the truth!" she blurted with a light chortle. "But seriously, San. He's a nice young man. Why don't you give him a chance? I only been here two seconds, and I can see that Leek loves him too."

"How you figure that and you only just got here?"

"When does that boy ever have two game controllers hooked up?" She placed her hands on her wide hips, a smirk etched on her beautiful deep chocolate face. I couldn't even deny her, but I didn't say nothing. "See! Not even when he has a friend over does he hook two controllers up. I'm telling you, baby. Leek likes Ju, and I believe you like him too."

"Mama…" I whined.

"Uh huh, I know, baby. I saw it a month ago, on the first Sunday you came back to church," she acknowledged.

"Wow, I didn't even realize it's been that long. Where has the time gone?" I pondered more to myself than her.

That didn't stop her from answering though. "Time has been wasting, baby. So what are you going to do about it?"

I didn't have an answer to that. The only thing I could do was see what happened… if anything happened. With the way I was stopping Ju's every advance, I was sure he would grow tired of it and move along.

I admit that, at first, I wanted him to do just that. I wanted him to find a new woman to pursue—to bother. I wasn't looking for love. If you asked me, I was happy, living my simple life with my son.

Once my mom and Leek left, I began to clear the table and wrap the food up. When I came back to the dining room to clean up, I found that Ju had already done it.

"Wow…" was all I could say as I gasped. *Jesus, he helps clean up too? You really laying it on thick, ain't you?*

"I hope you don't mind me doing the dishes." Ju came up from behind me. Feeling him this close had my center feeling overwhelmed again. It was like heat was pouring from his body to mine.

"No, I don't mind at all." I turned to face him. When I did, he reached in and his lips crashed into mine. It was so unexpected yet so… good. One part of me wanted to stop the kiss all together. The other part of me wanted to keep

71

going and see how far this would go. I was having a true tug of war with myself here.

"San…" Ju broke our kiss. "I'm sorry. I couldn't help myself. I been wanting to do that since you walked into my shop a month ago."

Again, he had my head spinning. I knew Ju liked me and wanted more than I was willing to give. I didn't know he'd been feeling me since his shop. "Wow, really?"

"Yeah, really, my love."

And there it was—that word. That perfect pet name he'd given me. *My love.* This time, I was the one who reached up and kissed *him!* I couldn't help myself. He was like a magnet. Plus, his lips were so nice.

"Mmm… Juuu!" A moan escaped my lips when he picked me up, and his lips fell on my neck. Feeling his lips on my skin really had me feeling some type of way.

I wanted him inside me as I started grinding my bottom half against him. When he sat down, I was sitting directly on his midsection. Feeling the bulging erection through his pants, I found myself grind against it through his jeans.

"Juwelz… ahh."

For a minute, he was into it. He was squeezing and rubbing my thighs and butt, pulling me closer to his hard on. Each time I felt it poke my center, I felt like I was losing my mind. I wanted this man right now so bad.

"San… San, San, San… stop." He stopped rubbing, kissing, and squeezing. I stared at him with a confused expression. Why was he stopping? "As bad as I want to do this, and I'm so attracted to you…" He shook his head. "We can't do this. Not yet and not like this."

"Then like what? We can go to my bedroom if you feel more comfortable with that." The words just fell from my lips. The shocked look on Ju's face was priceless. Hell, I was shocked myself.

"No, my love. That's not what I meant." He shook his head and helped me off his lap. I sat on the couch next to him, staring him patiently in the eyes. "I want to do this, but I promised myself if I ever went there with you, you'd be my wife first."

"W-wh-what?" I stood up on shaky legs. My hands went to my mouth. For some reason I couldn't understand, tears started filling up to the rim of my eyes and spilling over. Why am I crying right now? No, why am I not running for the hills or simply kicking him out? Why?

"I know that might sound a little over the top—"

"You think!" I didn't mean to raise my voice, but I was panicking. I had mixed emotions surging through me. I wanted to run, punch, and jump all over him, with feelings both of rage and love all at once. This man just told me he wanted to marry me! No, he promised himself he was going to marry me!

"San, I'm sorry. I didn't mean to scare you. I just wanted you to know. I can't and won't have sex with you until you're my wife."

"You say it as if I don't have a choice." I sat back down, calming myself down. "You want to marry me?" I had to hear him say that again. "Ju, we haven't even known each other that long. It's only been a month."

"I know it hasn't been that long. I'm a strong believer in *he who finds a wife, finds a good thing.* San, I believe you're my good thing. I want to be yours. I've told you before that I want to love you in every kind of way. I want to be there for you and Leek. Will you let me?"

Silence.

I heard him talking and honestly didn't know what to say. Everything was happening so fast. Not even a month ago, I was walking into this man's shop. Now he was sitting on my couch telling me that he wanted to marry me? God, is this really happening? Wake up me, send me a true sign, or something.

"San—"

"I need time and space to process this, Ju." I shook my head, staring at the floor.

"You got that, my love." He leaned over and kissed my forehead before standing and letting himself out of my apartment.

Jesus, I need you...

12

Juwelz

What was I thinking, telling San that I wanted to marry her? Man, I just knew that I screwed everything up between us. She probably thought I was sort of psycho now. Telling her I been wanting to kiss her from the day she walked in my shop? What the hell was I thinking? I wish there was a do over button so I could go back and not even kiss her soft lips. I would just proceed to watch the movie with her and have a good night.

"Hey, son! How did it go?" My dad was up, slowly walking from the kitchen and back to the living room. He had a tall glass of milk in one hand and a package of chocolate striped cookies under his armpit.

"Man, Pops…" I shook my head and plopped on the couch. "I think I screwed everything up," I shamefully admitted. There was no point on lying to my dad. He'd know sooner than later because he was going to see the change in my mood and demeanor.

"Ah, how so?" he asked after taking a seat in his La-Z-Boy.

"I told her I wanted to marry her." I felt defeated and

sounded even more defeated. "Now she's scared of me."
At least I felt like she was.

"Dang it, son. That girl got you proposing after a
month? You like her that much?" My pops was cracking
up. Good thing he didn't have a cookie in his mouth. He'd
probably choke on the crumbs if he did.

"I didn't propose to her. I just told her that I wanted to
marry her."

"It sounds like you proposed. You may as well have."
He popped a couple of cookies into his mouth. "How did
the topic come up?"

This time, I hung my head in shame. I hadn't talked to
my dad about sex in a long time. Not since I was thirteen.
"We um, were… we were about to take it to hit a homerun, and I stopped her in the process."

The next thing I knew, my dad was laughing hysteri-
cally. "Homerun, son? What am I, five? Boy, y'all was
about to have sex. Just say that… sex!"

"Okay. Yeah, Pop. We was about to go there." No
matter what he said, I still couldn't say it to him. It was
even hard to talk about. "I slowed her down and admitted
that I didn't want to go there with her until she was
my wife."

"Ahh, uh huh. I see now." He nodded.

"Yeah. Now I think I scared her and she ain't going to
talk to me anymore. I been beating myself up about it
since I left her place. I shouldn't have kissed her in the first
place."

"First mistake." Pops snapped his fingers and pointed
at me.

"Huh?"

"That was your first mistake. You never kiss a woman
unless you got plans to take it further."

"Huh?" See, now he really had me confused. Popping

a cookie in his mouth, he shook his head. "Pops, what kind of sense does that make?"

"Boy… okay, so you knew from jump you wanted to marry this woman. You took a good look at her and just knew——"

"It was more than just looking at her, Pop. I felt a connection like no other with her. Like a feeling that I wanted to follow her everywhere. I didn't know this woman from Adam or Eve, and I literally wanted to be where she was. That's how I know she my wife."

"Okay, son, but everybody knows that kissing leads to sex. It's human nature. If you didn't plan on taking that step, you shouldn't have been kissing."

"I couldn't help it. She was right there, and I was right there, and I just… went for it, Pop. I went for it and now look where that got us."

"Son, did she say she didn't want to talk to you? Did she give you some type of reason to believe she doesn't want you around her?"

"She told me she needed time and space to think. But I could tell she was terrified. At least, she looked to be."

"Women are complicated, son. She could've looked to be scared out her mind, but really… she thinking good things. She could be unsure of how she feels about you. It could be that you're ready and she's not. See, we're men. We tend to know what we want. Women… they're a little more complicated." He popped another two cookies in his mouth.

"I thought women were the ones who knew what they wanted, and men were the confused and complicated ones." At least that's what I heard.

"It goes both ways, son. In this case, you know what you want. Just give San some time to think it through.

She'll come around. In the meantime, pray, son. Pray for her and pray for yourself."

As I sat there, I let what my father said marinate. He wasn't doing nothing but telling the truth. Still, I couldn't help but to believe my own thoughts. I was going to give her some space though. I just prayed this space between us didn't become a permanent thing.

~&~

Three weeks later...

Hey, was thinking about you. Hope everything is good with you. I stared at the message, contemplating on sending it to San. It'd been three weeks since that night at her place, and I hadn't heard from or reached out. I was missing her. I knew she wanted space, but sheesh. She needed three weeks?

"I'm just going to send it. Why not? What's the worst that can happen?" Yes, I was talking to myself. I'd been sitting in my office almost two hours, thinking about what I'd say to San if she ever gave me another chance. I just needed one shot. If she didn't want to hear from me again, I'd leave her alone for good. I'd still cut Malik's hair for free, but I wouldn't bother her ever again. Yes, I'd been cutting Leek's hair for free. I hadn't told San that and I didn't plan on it. The only person that knew besides Cyn was Mama Jackson. She'd been the one bringing Leek in for his cuts. Matter of fact, he was due one. She didn't schedule an appointment, but I had a feeling they would be coming in sometime his week.

I looked forward to seeing Malik. I liked to hear how good he was doing in school. I hadn't bothered asking about his mom. Leek was a kid. He shouldn't be involved in what was going on between us. I wasn't one of them lame dudes who pulled stuff like that either.

Knock! Knock! Knock!

"Ju—whoa…" Cyn was coming into the room but stopped in the entrance. "You alright?"

"Huh? Am I alright? Why you ask me that?" I tried to play it off. I knew Cyn could see right through it though.

"Well for one, you looking like someone stole the puppy that you never had. Two, are you forgetting that I know you? I can always tell when something is off with you." She came fully into the room and shut the door. She took a seat in one of the plush chairs in front of my desk. "Tell me what's on your mind, bro."

"It's nothing, sis, really. I'm just sitting here chilling and waiting 'til my next client comes." I lied as I kept my eyes glued to my phone screen. It was stuck on the text I so badly wanted to send San. The text I so badly wanted to send and get an instant reply to. If only life worked like that.

"Mhm, you can't fool me. You're not a good liar. That's why you're an honest man. You say how and what you feel because it's always been hard for you to hold stuff in. This ain't nothing. You're going to tell me."

Aye, Cyn really was mad right now. She was used to me telling her everything because of how close we were. I couldn't help but start cracking up, laughing. Her pout face was so cute. She used to always do it when we were kids and she wasn't getting her way.

"It's not funny! Whatever! I don't even care no more. I only came in here to tell you that tonight is game night. Me, Cheyenne, and Aliyah got this new game and excited to play it." She clapped her hands, getting excited. "So don't forget, and bring my sis with you."

"*Your sis, huh?*" I lowly chuckled.

She mimicked me, laughing. "Yeah, *my sis*. Why you find that funny? I thought y'all were getting closer."

I shook my head. "Yeah, we were until I messed that up."

"What!" Cyn shot up from her seat.

"Will you lower your voice, Cynthia? Sheesh. The whole shop will hear you and come pressing their ears up against the door. Knowing Aaron, he'll walk right in." I didn't mean to snap so hard. Her exclamation caught me by surprise.

"Yeah, yeah, whatever." She waved me off. "So what happened? What did you do—ohhh!" She pointed at me as her hand went to cover her mouth. "That's what was wrong with you!"

I cut my eyes at her, tightening my jaw. "See? What I say? I knew it would come out sooner than later. So what did you do?"

"I told her I didn't want to have sex with her until we get married. By saying that, I think I scared her away."

"So she's mad you don't want to have sex until marriage?" Cyn screwed her face up.

"No, I didn't say that. I said that I scared *her* away. I told her that I was going to marry her."

"Okay, so what's the problem?"

"I. Scared. Her. Away."

"How? Because you want to marry her? That's crazy." Cyn shook her head. "Do you know how many women would love to hear that a man wanted to love and marry them? How we would feel so overwhelmed with joy and fear but still be so happy? Maybe she's just nervous or something. Give her some time. She'll come around."

"I've been doing that, and it's going on three weeks now." I pounded my fist on the desk, making Cyn jump back. "This is why I said I scared her away. I been giving her space. She hasn't called, texted, or nothing. She still sends Malik to get his hair cut, but I don't see or hear from her."

"Have you asked Malik or her mother about her? Maybe San is going through something, and you need to go see about her," Cyn tried to reason.

I shook my head. "No. If something was wrong, I'd know about it. Her mom doesn't say much, but that could be because San is telling her not to. I don't ask Leek because none of this should concern him. At least when me and his mom ain't getting along. I don't want him to ever have a reason to doubt. Especially after I told him that I like his mom."

"I think we should just go see about San," Cyn suggested.

"We? No, you mean me."

"No, I meant we. I like San too. I'm rooting for y'all."

"Thanks, sis." I softly smiled at her.

"Of course, bro. Now, fix it between y'all. Call her or text her." She stood to leave.

"I'll think about it."

"What kind of food do you want me to order for game night?" I was silently thanking God that she switched the topic.

"Order from Café Yummi. Get some of those bomb Spanish bowls you and Chey be eating from there. Water and wine sound good for the drinks?"

"Yep! I already had that part down." She giggled. "Okay, Café Yummi it is then."

"Sounds good." I nodded. I checked my phone to see what time it was. I had a client coming in later.

"Ju, I'm going to say this and then leave it alone." Cyn caught my attention. I didn't even know she was still there. Looking up at her, I gave her my attention. "Us women can be complicated sometimes. Even though we say stuff, we don't always mean it. Take San for instance. She said she needed time and space, which is true. I bet she's been staring at her phone, waiting for your call as bad as you want her to call you. I don't know. Maybe that's just me. Call her, bro. Work it out with her."

Everything Cyn just said sounded good. It wasn't that easy though. I was never afraid to show my true feelings to a woman. San, though, she was different. I saw that from the jump. Instead of saying anything verbally, I nodded my head and smiled.

Dear Lord, please help a brother out. I have feelings for San. Of course I want her feelings to mirror mine, but I can't force something that's not there. Please, Lord, if it's meant to be for us to be together... bring us back to each other. If not, then I'll have no choice but understand. Thank you, God. Amen.

13

Santana

Juwelz: Hey my love, I been thinking about you. I been missing you and just want to make sure you're all good. I know you said you needed your space. I just had to see about you though. I pray you're having a blessed day.

Staring at the text Ju just sent me, butterflies overtook my loins. I couldn't believe he was really texting me. I knew I told him I needed space, but honestly, I thought I scared him away by saying that.

That night, immediately after he left, I was kicking myself for acting the way I did. I just knew I had that man feeling stupid for telling me how he was feeling. Now I knew he was thinking about me. He was missing me. He wanted to see me. Silently, I thanked God that he had texted me first, because I didn't know what to say to him. I still didn't know what to say to him.

I guess the right thing to do was to tell him how I truly felt about him. How I'd been missing him like crazy. I wanted to see his face. I wanted to hear him call me his love. I wanted to kiss his lips, to feel him close to me.

"Next in line, please," I heard the lady at the counter

call out. I was standing in line, registering for my fall term classes. I was tired of going to class every day already, just standing in this line. I was happy that my new job allowed me to create my own schedule. I was able to take off when I wanted and work when I wanted. Having classes three days a week, I knew I was going to be tired. I was going to need all the rest that I could get. I planned on picking up the hours I'd lost during the week, on the weekends.

After getting everything squared away, I headed to pick Leek up from school. On my way there, I thought about the conversation we had last night. Leek really liked Juwelz. He asked for him all the time now. At first, it was annoying, but then I got over it. I just had my mom take him by the shop now.

After I told her what happened and how I was once again too embarrassed to show my face at the shop, she took pity on me. She agreed that she would take Leek to the shop if I agreed not to miss another Sunday at church.

As I was in line to pick up Leek, my phone started vibrating inside my purse. I was thinking it could've been *Visiting Angels* calling or sending texts and emails. They'd been on a roll lately. I guess caregivers had been calling out left and right.

When I picked up my phone, I noticed it was Cyn calling me. I only cringed because I didn't know why she was calling. We only texted a few times since we got each other's numbers.

Oh no, she must be calling about Juwelz! Ugh, see, I knew I shouldn't have gotten buddy-buddy too soon. These were my thoughts. The longer I held the phone in my palm, it seemed to vibrate longer and harder.

"Hello," I answered just in time.

"Hey, San, baby! How are you?" Cyn cheerfully inquired. A smile couldn't help but part my lips. Cyn was always so positive and nice. I couldn't be rude with her if I wanted.

"I'm okay. How are you?"

"Girl, I'm good! Listen, I called to invite you to the shop for a little kickback. It's just going to be a few of us here. Me, my girl Cheyenne, and her best friend, Aliyah. We're going to play games and do karaoke." She sounded so geeked. As fun as that sounded, I was on the fence. This wasn't even about Juwelz. I just hardly ever hung with a group of females. In my past, the ones I hung around were always petty and liked to throw shade on your situations. I didn't have time for it, so I stayed away from cliquey type of women.

"Ehh... Cyn, I'm not sure. I might have to work early tomorrow."

"Work? On a Saturday? Thought you had weekends off?" She sounded a little disappointed.

"I did, but I just started school, and I had to change my work schedule."

"Ohh... okay, boo! Maybe you can come next time. I really wish you could come tonight though. I'm ordering Café Yummi, and we're going to have some wine. We just got this new card game, and I'm geeked to play it."

"Aww, man... I really want to come, too." Really, there was no reason I couldn't go. I was just making up these excuses to keep my guard up. "Umm, let me think more on it. I might come anyways."

"Yay! Okay, I'll see you tonight at seven?"

"Seven it is. Should I bring anything?"

"No, ma'am. Just bring yourself. We'll have everything here already. I'm so excited that you're coming now! Okay, see you soon."

"Okay, see you soon." I laughed a little. Just as I got off the phone, Leek was getting in the car.

"Mama, was that Ju?" he anxiously asked.

"What makes you think it was Ju? Boy, I ain't always talking to Ju." I laughed, shaking my head. "Put your seat belt on."

"Oh, okay… I thought y'all were friends again," he solemnly answered. I glanced into the rear-view mirror and noticed he had his head down.

"Leek, why would you think that me and Ju are no longer friends?" I was feeling bad because my son seemed so disappointed.

"Because you guys don't hang out anymore. I thought he liked you and you liked him. He said he liked you."

"When did he tell you that?"

"When we went to Dave & Buster's. I asked him to take you out and to make you smile because you need to have fun too. He said he would do that. He lied to me." Leek seemed to be more angry than sad now.

"No, baby, he didn't lie to you. Ju wants to take me out and make me smile. I just been so busy and have to make time."

"Well, Mama, can you please let him put a smile on your face? I know he would be good at it. I mean, he's good at doing my hair. I know he'd be good at making you smile," Leek innocently reasoned. "Mama, I'm hungry. Can we go out to eat?"

Leek was now playing a game on his iPad. I quickly wiped the tears out of my eyes and cleared my throat before he noticed. "Yeah, baby, whatever you want."

Dear God, there is this man that I like a lot. My son likes him. He treats us good… just like I always prayed for. Now that I have him right in front of me, I'm afraid. I know that you did not give us the spirit of fear. So please help me to move forward, because I want to let this man love me in every kind of way. In Jesus name. Amen.

~&~

Okay, San. You got this. Just go in and be yourself. I took a deep breath, sitting inside my car, giving myself a mental pep talk. After some careful consideration, I decided to go to this kickback Cyn invited me to. I was praying that there weren't too many people. I didn't want to come across as awkward, if I was the only one in the room not saying anything. A part of me was hoping that Ju was in there.

"San! You made it!" Cyn greeted me when I came through the door. "Y'all, this is my sis, Santana. San, this is Cheyenne, and this is Aliyah." She introduced me to the beautiful women in the room. Both of them warmly smiled at me.

"Hey, girl!" they greeted in unison.

"Hey."

"You want some wine or water?" the one named Cheyenne asked. She was standing by the food and drinks, fixing a plate with fruit, crackers, and cheese on it.

"Water is fine with me." I wasn't much of a drinker. Plus, like I said, I didn't know these women like that. I didn't want to be getting too loose around them just yet.

"Okay, boo! Aliyah, water or wine?"

"Wine, girl! The day I had today was just..." She shook her head, staring at the floor. "Tragic."

"What happened?" we all seemed to ask at the same time.

"This woman, y'all. I've never seen someone be so cruel to a man that's just trying to do right by his daughter. She doesn't want him to have custody because he doesn't want to be with her. So she took him to court to get full custody. It's so sad, y'all."

"Wow, that's crazy. I can't stand a bitter woman like that. Especially when you have a man that wants to be there for his child. All because he don't want you, you go and hurt him by taking the child away. Man, I'm praying for that woman and that man." Cheyenne shook her head.

"Aliyah is a lawyer, San," Cyn informed me.

I loved how she wanted me to stay in the loop so I wouldn't be lost. That told me that she was genuine. Not that I ever had any doubt.

"Aww, okay. I'm sorry you had to go through that, Aliyah."

Aliyah shook her head. "I see cases like this all the time. The mothers be having good men as fathers for their kids. They want the man but the man don't want them. So they go hurt the man by any means necessary."

"Meanwhile, us women who baby daddies ain't ish, wishing we had a man that was willing to step up to the plate. Nowadays, you had to watch these men that wanted to get with single mothers. You never know if they have ulterior motives," Cheyenne spat in disgust. She had a point.

It made me think about Ju. He was a good man, and he wanted to be in me and my son's life. Ju wasn't on any type of weird stuff though. He was genuine.

"How many kids do you have?" I asked, taking a sip of water.

"Girl, I have a set of eight-year-old twins. A boy and a girl, Kaylynn and Kaydence. You have kids?"

"Yeah, I have an eight-year-old son. His name is Malik."

"This is my baby, Riley. She's eight as well." Aliyah showed us a picture on her phone.

"Okay, so great. I have two nieces and two nephews and they're all eight," Cyn joked, causing us all to laugh. As the conversation continued to go around, I started to feel comfortable. These ladies were open books. I found out a little bit about all of them.

Cyn was twenty-six, single, and didn't have any kids. She told us about how she was going to school at Everest and got ripped off. I felt so bad for her. I would be hurt if something like that had happened to me. The good thing was, she got all her money back. She was working in the shop until she figured out what she wanted to do next.

Aliyah was twenty-seven, a single mother, and a family court lawyer. She spent a lot of time helping her clients keep custody of their kids. She also worked with a lot of social workers. Her excuse for not having a man was that she didn't have time for one right now. I could relate to her in that sense. Although I wanted Ju, I feared not being enough when it came down to spending time. She also revealed to us that she'd lost Riley's dad to a tragic accident while she was pregnant and entering her junior year of college. Now that, I couldn't relate to. I felt for her though.

Lastly, Chey was twenty-four, a beautician with a set of boy-girl twins, and in a complicated relationship with her child's father. He was currently in jail, serving three years for domestic violence and burglary. Chey admitted that she still loved him, but she didn't think she should still be with him.

After hearing a little of everyone's story, I had to get me a glass of wine. Knowing a little about everyone made me put my own guards down. When it was my turn to tell about me, I didn't hold too much back. By the end of my story, we were passing a box of tissues around. It wasn't that my story was super sad. I started crying as I told them how I fell in love with a man that had no real intentions of being a part of my life. He just wanted my innocence for bragging rights. When I got pregnant, he flaked. That was one of the reasons I wasn't trying to get serious with anyone. I was afraid that they'd leave me like Isaac did.

"Wow, y'all. I'm so happy we did this. Y'all don't know how good it felt to just get that out," I admitted, wiping my tears. I felt like a big weight had lifted off my shoulder. I was no longer holding that stuff in. It was crazy how all you needed to do was talk about stuff in order to feel better. *Thank you, God*, I mentally thanked Him. If I didn't come here tonight, I probably wouldn't be feeling the way I felt, acting how I was.

"Aww, I'm just happy you came, girl." Cyn laughed as she wiped the last of her tears.

"No, I'm happy the guys decided not to stick around." Aliyah rolled her eyes to the ceiling with a smirk.

"Mhm, girl! You know you wanted to see your boo, Sean!" Chey called her out, making us all laugh. I wasn't sure which one was Sean, but I assumed he was someone that worked in the shop. Chey being the only woman, Ju had a lot of men barbers.

"Girl, ain't nobody thinking about that man! Just because I said he was a good dad to his daughter, doesn't mean that I like him like that!" Aliyah defended herself. I saw right through that smirk though.

"Mhm, girl! I don't know why Cyn laughing. She just happy to have gotten rid of Aaron!" Chey was on a roll.

Cyn stopped laughing and got serious. "Ohh, I swear I can't stand his nasty butt! He always trying to mack." She rolled her eyes.

"Didn't I hear him say that he'd give up all his playa ways if you just gave him a chance?" Chey giggled.

"Girl, you know you did, and I don't believe that not one bit. I bet he got a bunch of babies he knows nothing about."

"Giiirllaa! By who! All these old women he be talking about? I doubt they can have any more kids."

"Ohh, that's wrong, Chey!" Aliyah exclaimed.

"Girl, it's only wrong if it's a lie. You should see these women he be talking about. It's like he's using them for their money, girl." Chey continued to spill the tea. I didn't know if what she was saying was true or not. If we were talking about the same Aaron, I believed it.

"See, I had to tell Ju about the things that Aaron says around Malik. Had my baby coming home talking about getting a girlfriend. Y'all, I almost had a heart attack!"

"Whaaaat!" they all exclaimed after me telling them that.

"Mhm." I sipped my wine. I was feeling nice and toasted. I was still on my first glass and halfway through. I wasn't a drinker, so a small sip could have me feeling something.

"So, what's up with y'all anyways? I wasn't going to call you out, but, girl..." Chey was holding her chest, cracking up. "You rolled up in here and let Ju *have it*! I will never forget that day. I never asked what that was about, and Ju wouldn't tell us either."

"He didn't?" I was shocked to hear that. I was sure that he had told everyone in the shop.

"Girl, nope! He told us to mind our business and get back to work," Chey revealed. "So, now that he not here, y'all together or what?"

"Girl, it's complicated." I shook my head.

"Complicated how?" Aliyah inquired.

"Well, Ju—well, no, *I* have been giving him a hard time. He wants to date me, and I constantly turn him down. I like him, like, a lot, but..." I shook my head.

"But what, sis? Ju is a good guy. He'd never do you like your ex did. Every time Leek comes into the shop, his eyes light up as if he was his own. I know that's my cousin/brother and all, so you can argue I'm a little bias. If Ju wasn't ish, trust, I wouldn't be standing here vouching for him."

"Right, and I'll say this. When I was fresh out of hair school, none of these shops would give me a chance. We only have a select few black shops around here, and none of them had room for me. I went to some other places I thought would hire me, but nope." Chey shook her head. "I ran into Juwelz at the perfect time, and he took a chance on me. This was back when this was only a place for men to come get their hair cut. Ju helped me get myself out there. He promoted me on his Instagram and on the website. He showed me how to advertise right, and now, I have so many clients I don't have enough time in the day to get everybody done in a week. Ju is truly a godsend."

"Yup, he sure is. Family or not, he didn't have to let me do his books. I'm not even finished getting my degree in accounting. Yet, here I am. I thank God for him."

Listening to Chey and Cyn's testimonies about St. Juwelz had me placing him on a higher pedestal than he already was. I knew you weren't supposed to praise man. I wasn't doing that, but I was praising God for him.

"Thank you, guys, for this night. I truly appreciate it. I also needed it," I admitted.

"Girl, we glad you came!" Cyn cheered. "But! You will think about what we said about Ju, right?" The hope in her voice was so cute, it tickled me.

"Yeah, girl. I'll definitely keep it in mind."

Thank you, God, for sending these beautiful ladies into my life. You knew what you were doing!

14

Juwelz

It was a little after nine when I finally got into the house. I was just coming from Chili's, having dinner and drinks with Aaron and Sean. We decided at the last minute to skip out on game night with the ladies and do our own thing. Cyn was upset at first. She got over it after Aaron did whatever he did to annoy her on the daily.

I admit that this time with my bros was much needed. It was good to just unwind, talk, and have a couple of beers. Before going our separate ways, we agreed that we'd do this every few weeks. It was good to get certain things off our chests with just us men.

"Hey, Juwelz!" Brittany was coming from the back. I already knew she had just helped my dad to bed. The TV in the front room was off, and his throw blanket was folded and placed neatly in his chair.

"Hey, Britt. I apologize for being late. You know how it is when you having a good time." I apologized as I took my wallet out and pulled a few twenties out. "Here, take this as a token of gratitude and a part of my apology."

"Oh, no, I can't." Brittany shook her head.

"I know it's company policy, but please, take this." I placed it in her palm and closed it.

"Wow, Juwelz. I don't know what to say. Thank you so much!" Brittany gushed as tears filled up to the rim of her eyes and spilled over. "You're such a blessing."

"You're the true blessing, Britt." I patted her back as I opened the door for her to leave. Before she did, she gave me a tight hug around the waist. Brittany was so much shorter than me, so you can imagine how she was hugging me. I placed my arm around her shoulders and gave them a gentle squeeze.

"See you tomorrow, Ju." Britt waved.

"*See you tomorrow, Ju,* huh?" San startled both Britt and I. "Wow, and to think I was coming over here to talk about us." She shook her head and turned on her heels to walk away.

"San! Wait up!" I went after her. I noticed how she was walking, and immediately, I knew she was intoxicated.

Catching up to her, I grabbed her around the waist before she could open her car door. She started to pull and push away from me. I had a good grip on her though. "San, chill, love."

"Get off of me, Ju! Go back to your little girlfriend!" She was trying hard to break free.

"Seriously, San? Chill out before you really hurt yourself." I got her to stop squirming long enough to make her look at me. She was staring at me with a hard glare. I didn't care about that. I just wanted her to calm down. "Brittany isn't my girlfriend. She's my dad's caregiver. She was just leaving for the night."

"Then why were y'all all hugged up?" San boldly queried. Shaking my head, I did my best to hold back my laugh. San was jealous right now, and it was cute.

"Come in the house and let's talk, my love."

"No. Not until you tell me why y'all were hugged up," she slurred.

"San, how did you manage to get here so under the influence. Where are you coming from right now?"

"The shop—your shop. I was with the ladies. After we went our separate ways, I came to see you... I miss you, Ju," she babbled.

"I miss you too, beautiful. Come on, let's go inside the house." I scooped her up bridal style and carried her into the house. "Ju-Ju, I'm sorry. I miss you so much. I want to marry you too... right now. You my man. I love you, Ju. I love you so much."

She was just rambling on and on as I helped her change into a pair of my boxers and a t-shirt. I never imagined San being this cute while being drunk. She was saying all types of goofy stuff and giggling. As much as I wanted to be mad at Cyn, Chey, and Liyah, I couldn't. I was more praising God because San came to my house. She could've ended up anywhere but here. Now she was professing her undying love for me. Yeah, I was basking in it. However, I knew she was under the influence. They said that was when the truth really came out. We'd see in the morning though.

"Ju, I want you." San was propped up on the bed as I came back into the room. I had put her clothes in the wash so she could have something fresh in the morning.

"San, baby, lay down and get some sleep. You tipsy as hell." I got on the bed with her. She surprised me when she climbed on top of me and started kissing me. I could taste and smell the pink Moscato on her breath.

"San, chill, mama. Cut it out. Lay down and get some rest."

"I'm not sleepy. I'm horny, and I want you, Ju." She was now grinding and kissing on me. "Ju, can I have you?"

"You already got me, baby. Now lay down." As bad as I wanted to give her what she was begging for, I meant what I said. I wasn't having sex with San until she became my wife. Not only that, but she was intoxicated.

"Juuu!" She whined in a baby voice as I lifted her up and tucked her into bed. "Ju, I want you. You don't want me?" Her eyes were closed as she continued to mumble. "I love you."

"I love you too, my love," I whispered in her ear and kissed her forehead.

Thank you, Lord, for bringing her back to me…

~&~

When I woke up, San wasn't laying there anymore. I peeked over at the clock and saw that it was just turning nine o'clock in the morning. I picked my phone up off the nightstand to see if maybe she had texted or called. I didn't know if she had left early this morning or in the middle of the night. A twinge of worry pinched my chest as I called her phone.

"Good morning, my love." She sounded all perky and awake, like she wasn't just sleeping her buzz down in my bed last night.

"Well good morning to you, too. How come you didn't wake me before you left. I could've made sure you got home safely." I felt myself getting riled up and had to calm down. This woman didn't know how much I truly cared for her.

She giggled into the receiver, causing my already tight mood to get a little tighter. She wasn't taking me seriously. "Yeah, well I'm glad you made it home safely."

"Ju, are you—"

Yup, I hung up on her. I was that mad. Call it petty or what you want. I was in my chest. I was tired of San treating me like some type of joke.

A part of me wanted to call her back and apologize to her. Then again, I wanted her to call me for a change. She was saying all this mess about her loving me. She was going to have to show me something.

After getting my hygiene together, I went to get my dad up. I didn't feel like cooking breakfast this morning. So we were going out to Denny's.

"Pop?" Peeking in his room, I didn't see him in his bed. That was unusual because he normally needed help in the morning. His legs would either be too stiff to move sometimes, or they'd to shaky.

Walking further into the room, I was checking to see if maybe he fell. Next, I checked his bathroom. He wasn't there either. Scratching my head, I left the room. I was already a little ticked because of San. I didn't want to take it out on him.

"Pop! Where you at?" I called out.

"We down here, son!" he yelled back. *We?* I thought as the smell of fresh coffee and bacon caressed my nostrils.

"Good morning, Julius." San didn't sound as perky as she did earlier. She was standing over the stove, scrambling up eggs. My heart skipped a beat as I stared at her beautiful morning glow. She was still in the shirt and boxers I had given her to wear.

"San, I didn't know you were still here. I thought you went home and... I don't know what I was thinking hanging up on you like that. I was wrong, and I apologize."

"Mhm, I forgive you. You hungry?" She was dividing eggs between three plates.

Next, she opened the oven and pulled out a pan full of

warm sausage, bacon, biscuits, and home fried potatoes. "Why you still standing there?"

"No reason." I went to sit and wait at the table with my dad. He smelled like he'd already showered, and he was changed into his outfit for the day.

"What time did you get up, Pop?" I inquired to make conversation.

"Son, I was up at seven thirty. San came and helped me get ready after she heard me struggling. You were chopping logs," he joked.

"Aw man, I'm sorry about that, Pop."

"Don't be sorry to me. Tell that beautiful woman in there sorry. She got to listen to that and try to sleep though it for the rest of her life." He winked and laughed. I joined him in laughter, shaking my head.

"I sure hope you're right, Pop," I replied just as San came into the room and placed our plates in front of us. The food looked and smelled good. Who needed Denny's when you had a Santana in your kitchen? I was so used to cooking all the meals that I forgot how it felt to be served by someone else. Before San came to join us, she made sure we had everything we needed. I was now seeing what my pops meant by her reminding him of my mom. It was scary and comforting all in one. I could also see how it made him miss her. My mom used to take care of my dad and me the same way San was doing now. I didn't blame him for cancelling her as a caregiver.

Ten minutes after we started to eat, my dad broke the silence. "San, baby, I just want to apologize for how I left things between us. I should have explained things before making that call. I know it also put a strain on you and my son's relationship."

"I appreciate that, JD, and I accept your apology. Why

did you cancel me as your caregiver, by the way—if you don't mind me asking?"

"Well, because you remind me a lot of my wife. Having you here those couple of days, I began to miss her like I haven't before. I didn't realize it was because you were here until you left."

I could see the mixed emotions cross San's face. "Oh wow, I'm so sorry. I had no idea, JD."

"I know, sweetheart, and it's all good now. Seeing you and my son's relationship restored makes me so happy. I know y'all will love just as hard as his mama and me did."

Simultaneously, San and I caught each other's gazes. I smiled at her, and she smiled back. No words were needed. It was like we already knew.

After breakfast, I helped San clear the table and clean up. My dad went to sit in his favorite spot and watch TV.

"San." We were just about done with the dishes.

"Yes?" she answered sweetly.

"Do you remember what happened last night?" I wanted to see if any of what she said was real, or was she just really bent and didn't mean it.

She stopped what she was doing to look at me. "Of course I do. I appreciate you for being so respectful, too."

"You don't have to thank me for that. I'm always going to treat with respect. You're a queen; you deserve it."

"I meant what I said last night too."

I smirked. "Well you said a whole lot of stuff last night, my love."

I saw the smile creep up on her face. "You know what I mean."

I shook my head. "No, San, I don't. This whole time I've been showing and telling how I feel. You have yet to do so. Except when you're pushing me away. You show up here last night, go off on the caregiver, intoxicated and professing your love for me, after not speaking to me for three whole weeks. Now you're down here in my kitchen, cooking breakfast, telling me *I know what you mean.* Tell me what you mean, San, because I don't know nothing."

"Ju—I, uh…" She paused when I came and got into her personal bubble. I had her cornered between the wall and my chest now.

"You what?"

"I love you, Ju," she blurted. "I know how I've been acting, but I couldn't help it. For eight years, it's just been me and my son. When his dad left me while I was pregnant, I hurt. My family turned their backs on me. People I thought would always be there just left me. The only person that's been solid is my mama. So I'm careful with me. I don't like letting people in. Then here you come. The perfect stranger, all nice and… fine…" She gasped, biting her bottom lip and eyeing me up and down. I burst into laughter as she checked me out. "You make me feel like I can trust you. You make me feel like I can love again. You make me want to love again, Ju. I won't lie to you though… I'm terrified that I'll get hurt. I'm also terrified that if I don't take this leap that I'll miss out on a real shot at love."

"San, I can't promise you anything. I will say that it's not my intention to hurt you. I would never do anything to intentionally make you feel bad. I won't lie to you either. I'm equally terrified. I haven't been in a real relationship in… years! I just know that when I look at you, my heartbeat speeds up. When you enter a room, I could lose all the breath out my body. When you leave, I want to follow you. When I look into your eyes, I want to love away all the pain you've been through. I want to show you that love is here for you, baby. I can be the one you love. It's just all up to what you want."

I helped her wipe her face as the tears poured from her eyes. "So what's it going to be, my love?"

"I want to love you in every kind of way," she admitted, smiling through the tears. That was all I needed to hear as I took her face and mashed my lips into hers.

God, I thank you...

15

Santana

A year later…

"*This ain't a dream. You're here with me. Boy, it don't get no better than you.*" I heard the music softly playing as I stood outside of the church, waiting my turn to go inside.

Shaking my head, I laughed at Cyn and Aaron as they approached me. As always, Aaron was busy shooting his shot while Cyn shot him down and fussed at him. If they stopped arguing long enough, they'd see how good they looked together.

I admired the way they looked in their matching colors and attire. Cyn was wearing a floor-length wild orchid colored gown. Aaron was wearing a black suit with a rose the same color as her dress in his upper jacket pocket.

"San, you know you my girl, but I'm still going to get you for this," Cyn joked as she came over and hugged me.

"Nah uhh, blame your cousin. He picked Aaron as his best man. He could've picked anybody else." I was so tickled. The minute I told Ju I was going to ask Cyn to be my maid of honor, he went and asked Aaron to be his best man. He knew he was wrong, knowing they had to walk down the aisle together. I told him to pick someone else, but he wasn't budging. Aaron was his best friend.

"Thanks, sis. Tell me how you really feel." Aaron added his two cents. Me and him now shared a love hate sibling relationship. He got on my nerves, and I got on his. I had forgiven him for trying to turn my son into a mini player.

"Whatever, bro. You know it's all love. Can y'all just fake like y'all love each other for today? For me? Please?"

"Love?" Cyn spat in question.

"*Like!*" I quickly corrected.

"Yeah, for you I will. Come on, big head. Don't be trying to feel on my booty either!" Cyn griped at him as they went into the sanctuary together. Aaron was trying to hold Cyn's hand, but she wasn't having it. I swear they couldn't get along for nothing.

Next, Sean and Aliyah walked up together. Aliyah and Cheyenne's dresses were similar to Cyn's. They were the same color but just below the knees, and the straps were the off the shoulder type.

"Hey, beautiful!" Sean and Aliyah both sang at the same time. They were both smiling at me like this was their special day.

I was tickled at Liyah's words to me during rehearsal. She thought it was cute and funny how everybody got paired up. Again, I blamed it all on Ju. He had more friends than I did. He could've had any of his boys to do these roles. All I had was Cyn, Chey, and Liyah. Over the year, we'd gotten a lot closer. These weren't just women I occasionally saw anymore. These were my sisters. We met up every other weekend now to have dinner and drinks. I loved them so much, and I knew it was mutual.

"Heeeey, San, baby! Gurl, you look so beautiful!" Chey

came and hugged me. Even in heels, she was a little shorter than me.

"Thank you, babe. You look beautiful too." Chey was walking down the aisle by herself. Ju only wanted Aaron and Sean in the wedding, so that left Chey to walk alone. She wasn't upset about it. She actually was the one who suggested that Liyah and Sean walk together.

"Aww! You guys look so cute!" I gushed over Riley and Kaydence in their flower girl dresses. Leek and Kaylynn were right behind them in their little suits. Leek was carrying the rings and Kaydence had the broom.

As the doors opened, the kids started to slowly walk in. "Now I know you weren't about to walk down that aisle without me."

"JD!" I rushed over into his arms and hugged him. He was fully standing without his cane, looking dapper as ever.

Tears overwhelmed my eyes and face as I thought about his journey to walk without the cane. Man, God is so good. Here was this man that I met, he was in a wheelchair for the longest, until one day he decided he'd use a cane.

When I found out that he never wanted to use the cane until I came along, I cried like a baby. I was witnessing how God could use us to be a difference and blessing in each other's lives. A year ago, around the same time Ju and I made everything official with us, JD decided he wanted to do therapy. He wanted to get back his life and live it. To see him standing without the cane, ready to walk me down the aisle, had me so emotional.

"You ready to do this?" He held his arm out for me to take.

I took a deep breath. "Ready as I'll ever be."

"Love… so many things I've got to tell you. But I'm afraid I don't know how. 'Cause there's a possibility you'll look at me differently…"

When I noticed it was Ju singing, I stopped where I stood, and I lost it. I would've fell to the floor as I broke down crying, but JD was holding onto me tightly. He wouldn't dare let me go and fall to the ground.

"Ever since the first moment I spoke your name, from then on, I knew that by you being in my life, things were destined to change 'cause... love... so many people use your name in vain." Ju continued to sing as he walked toward me.

I wasn't even halfway down the aisle, and he was coming to me. *Jesus, where you make this man at?* I thought as I remembered him telling me one day that he'd always meet me more than halfway.

I wanted to run the rest of the way to him, but I was stuck in my stance, shaking and crying. I was so over-whelmed by my emotions. When he got to me, he grabbed my hand and we walked the rest of the way to the altar together.

"Through all the ups and downs, the joy and hurt... love. For better or worse I still will choose you first..." There wasn't a dry eye in the room by the time he was finished singing.

"The couple has prepared their own vows." Even the pastor was choked up. "Santana, you say yours then Julius will say his." We nodded in understanding.

"Ju..." I choked on tears. "I first want to say that I love you so much. This past year, you've shown me what true love is. I love how you respect me and my son. I love how you stepped up to the plate to teach Leek things when you didn't have to. I love the way you smile at me. You make me feel like the prettiest girl in the world. I looked up what a true king is, and, baby, you're it. A king loves uncondi-tionally, shows mercy, and honors those he loves. That's you, baby... my king. I promise to love you through the good times and the bad. Through sickness and health, I will be by your side. You do so much for us that I don't mind doing anything for you. I love you."

Before he started, he leaned down and kissed my lips so passionately, I felt my whole body going numb with lust for him. "San, my love. You've made me a better man than I was a year ago. You're so patient and understanding with me. You listen to me talk about my dreams and visions. I love that so much. Your laugh is music to my soul. Your smile makes my day brighter. I look at you like you're the only woman in the world because you're the only woman I need. Baby, you're everything I need and want in a woman. I thank God for you daily. I'm going to always treat Leek like my own because he's just that... He's my son."

Ju choked up, staring at Leek. I glanced over at Leek, and he was crying too. The mama bird in me reached my hand out for him, and he came and stood next to me. "Ahh... San, baby, thank you. Thank you for being the queen that you are. I promise to love and cherish you through everything we go through. I'll continue to meet you more than halfway. All you got to do is show up."

"I'll always show up, baby!" I blurted out, causing light laughter to erupt around the room.

"May we have the rings?" the pastor asked Leek. He pulled them out his pocket and handed them to us. Ju and I slipped them on and were kissing before the pastor could fully officiate us.

"Ladies and gentlemen, I present Mr. and Mrs. Julius 'Juwelz' Davis," he announced as we jumped the broom.

Everyone was cheering and clapping all around us as we continued to kiss and hug. This day, this moment was everything I wanted it to be. I couldn't do anything but give God praise for this man he placed in my path.

When I met Juwelz, I didn't think we'd be right here

right now. This wasn't in my plans. Had it been up to me, Leek and I would've walked out that shop and never looked back. It was funny... There was this saying that went like this: If you want to hear God laugh, tell him your plans. I probably had him cracking him up!

God, I thank you...

The End!

Facebook: Brii Taylor
Facebook Page: Ms. Brii
Facebook Group: Ms. Brii's Reader's Group
Instagram: everything_ms.brii
Twitter: taylor_brii
SC: Bribby_monroe
Website: www.msbrii.com
Email: briitaylorwrites@gmail.com

COMING SUNDAY!

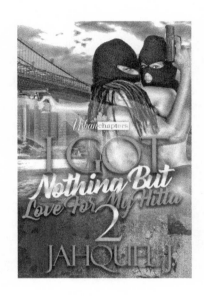

CPSIA information can be obtained
at www.ICGtesting.com
Printed in the USA
LVHW110534300719
625730LV00004BA/838/P

9 781072 023395